# Rachel SINCLAIR
# SECRETS AND LIES

## By Rachel Sinclair

Kansas City Legal Thrillers

*Bad Faith*
*Justice Denied*
*Hidden Defendant*
*Injustice for All*
*L.A. Defense*
*The Associate*
*The Alibi*
*Reasonable Doubt*
*The Accused*
*The Hate Crime*
*Secrets and Lies*
*Until Proven Guilty*

Vinci Books

vinci-books.com

Published by Vinci Books Ltd in 2026

1

Copyright © Rachel Sinclair 2018

The author has asserted their moral right to be identified as the author of this work in accordance with the Copyright, Designs and Patents Act 1988. This work is a work of fiction. Names, characters, places and incidents are the product of the author's imagination or are used fictitiously. Any resemblance to actual persons, living or dead, places and incidents is entirely coincidental.

All rights reserved. No part of this publication may be copied, reproduced, distributed, stored in any retrieval system, or transmitted in any form or by any means, including photocopying, recording, or other electronic or mechanical methods, nor used as a source for any form of machine learning including AI datasets, without the prior written permission of the publisher.

The publisher and the author have made every effort to obtain permissions for any third party material used in this book and to comply with copyright law. Any queries in this respect should be brought to the attention of the publisher and any omissions will be corrected in future editions.

A CIP catalogue record for this book is available from the British Library.
Paperback ISBN: 9781036703257

The EU GPSR authorised representative is Logos Europe, 9 rue Nicolas Poussion, 17000 La Rochelle, France
contact@logoseurope.eu

## Chapter One

I GOT into the office and saw a man sitting on the couch. He was an elegant man - dressed in a high-dollar suit and red silk tie, with wing-tipped leather shoes buffed to a high-gloss shine. He had a head of dark wavy hair and light eyes, like those of Benedict Cumberbatch. He was sitting with his legs crossed, one over the other, and, when I walked in, he glanced at me, but did not smile.

Nor did he get up.

I had no idea why he was sitting there.

I looked over at Pearl quizzically. She knew my expressions and could read what I wanted without my saying a word. She cleared her throat. "Silas Porter," she said, motioning to the man on the couch. "He, uh, didn't have an appointment."

I looked over at the man, who was now staring at me. With those penetrating, super-light eyes and an expression that belied exactly nothing, I felt just a little creeped out. I looked down at my arm and saw the hairs standing on end. In prison, I met guys that gave me the creeps like this one did. They were usually the psychos, the guys who had no conscience and could kill you with a smile on their face. I tended to steer clear of guys like the ones I knew in prison, although I sometimes took them on as clients, as I loved a challenge. Still, I was just a little bit pissed, because the guy had just barged on in the office without an appointment. I had things to do that afternoon. Didn't this guy know how busy attorneys are? Maybe he just didn't care.

"Hello, Mr. Harrington," he said, finally speaking in a booming voice. "I'm very sorry I came to see you without calling ahead."

"Uh, it's okay," I lied. "I have a deposition in an hour, and court appearances after that, so I have a few minutes to talk to you." As I looked at him, I couldn't help but feel there was just something so familiar about his face. I couldn't quite place it. As I stared at him, a vague kernel entered my mind. There was something in the news about Silas Porter. It was something I'd glanced at in the morning before I began my day. I seemed to remember reading something about how he had been arrested for murdering his wife, Ava. The story, however, was hazy, nebulous.

"Mr. Porter," I said to him. "I hope you don't mind, but I need to take a few minutes. I'll call you in when I'm ready to see you." I had no idea why I didn't just throw the guy out of the office, but I had to admit, I knew he probably had the money to pay a big fee and I had kids to feed at home.

I could see in those light eyes a hint of disapproval. It seemed he wanted to speak with me right at that very second, even though I wasn't ready for him at all. He stared at me briefly and put his finger to his cheek. And then he nodded ever-so-slightly. "As you wish," he said curtly.

What the hell? He's going to give me attitude, even

though he was the one inconveniencing me, not the other way around? Also, I couldn't shake the cold feeling I felt being in this guy's presence. I shook my head as I walked towards my office. I got in to the door of my suite, sat down and brought out my newspaper. I scanned it, and it wasn't long before I found the story I was looking for – apparently that elegant man who just addressed me so formally had, to put it mildly, a freaky side to him. At least, according to this paper, he did. The story in the paper was about how Silas apparently killed his wife, but, according to him, he didn't mean to do it.

As I read the article in the newspaper, I decided I probably didn't want to have a thing to do with this guy. Not only because the article portrayed him as abusive to his wife, but also because this case was on the front page, and that meant media attention I just didn't want.

Silas was apparently a billionaire by the age of 32. He had founded a tech firm out in the Silicon Valley five years ago, and it just went public, which made him one of Silicon Valley's newest billionaires. He and his wife, Ava, who apparently came from old money, and was a multimillionaire in her own right, were in Kansas City for a tech conference at the time of Ava's death. Ava's family was from this area, so Silas and Ava apparently maintained a home in the Hallbrook area, a tony area in Leawood, Kansas, where sports stars, CEOs, and other wealthy individuals lived.

I read on and found out a guest house behind the couple's main house apparently burned to the ground with Ava inside. The conflagration was so sudden and violent that Ava's body was burned to the point that there was nothing left of her except for her two hands.

I shuddered as I thought about the possibility that Ava burned to death inside that house. I couldn't think of anything more agonizing than that. I closed my eyes and pictured the searing pain she must have felt as the flames hit her and I shuddered. At the same time, I wondered why Silas would've been charged with murdering her. It sounded like the fire that trapped Ava was accidental.

As I read on, I got the answer to that question. Apparently at the time of the fire, Ava was chained to a wall, and the police found accelerant at the scene, so Silas was also being charged with arson.

Ava was apparently helpless, unable to avoid the flames because she had no means of escaping. After reading this, I immediately prejudged the case. I wouldn't take this guy. No way, no how. Not for all the money in the world. And he had all the money in the world, so he really didn't need me to represent him.

I summoned him into my office and he sat down across from me. True to form, he just stared at me. Waiting for me to speak with him.

"Mr. Porter," I began. "I thank you for coming in here, although I'm not quite sure why you came in here without making an appointment first, but that's neither here nor there. But I'm afraid this is not a case I'm going to want. Now, I would refer you to some other criminal defense attorneys in the area, people I know, but I'm quite sure you have at your disposal access to the most expensive hired guns in the city. I don't think you'll need my referrals."

Silas sat across from me, still not say anything. Then, after a few minutes, he finally spoke. "Mr. Harrington," he began. "I understand you probably have your own views of the case. After all, the media tends to be very one-sided in these things. And, my wife, Ava, her family is very well-to-do. Very old money in the area. They've never liked me. They don't like anybody who's new money. And they're convinced I murdered her in cold blood. They're controlling the story. Of course, I'm changing that today. My publicist is getting in touch with the newspaper and my side of the story will dominate the headlines from now on."

"Well then, I guess you'll be just fine. You'll get some kind of high-dollar lawyer on the case, your publicist will control the narrative, and everything will turn out great." I wondered how his stock was doing. After all, when something like this happens to the CEO of a major multinational corporation, the stock prices usually plunge. If that was the case, the guy probably lost millions of dollars overnight. Of course, losing millions of dollars overnight pales in comparison to losing your freedom and your livelihood, which was what this guy was facing.

"Mr. Harrington," he said. "I don't think you understand. I'm determined I'm going to hire you as my attorney. You are right about one thing – I have access to any lawyer I want. This is the kind of case that can make a career. That said, I have access to lawyers who already have a stellar career. Attorneys who have tried cases much more high-profile than this one. But I want you. Only you."

That was weird. I had no clue why he wanted to hire me so desperately. I had some high-profile cases of my own in the past but they were all local. I'd never been involved with something this high-profile. I certainly was not a hired-gun celebrity attorney in any way, shape or form, which was what this guy probably should've hired. I wasn't a nobody, but I certainly wasn't a somebody either.

It was my turn to stare. "I'm not sure I understand. I'm telling you I don't want the case. Full stop. I've got enough on my plate and I don't want to get involved in something that'll lead to me being hounded by the pap. I'm not quite sure why that message isn't getting through."

"I think you will want this case once you hear my side of the story. And please hear me out. That's all I ask of you. An hour of your time, and I think you'll want this case."

"As I said earlier when you first came into the office, I have a deposition in an hour. So –"

"Then I shall return this evening. At what time do you have free in the late afternoon or early evening?"

I sighed. I had to admit to being intrigued on why this guy was so adamant to hire me. And maybe I shouldn't prejudge it so much. I could listen to his story and kick him out the door. I owed him that much.

"I don't like taking clients in the evening because I have two kids at home who need me to feed them and get on them about doing homework and that sort of thing. So…" I sighed. I didn't want this guy. But at the same time, I had to find out why he wanted me so badly, and I had to admit the prospect of being able to charge $500 an hour, and get it with no problem, was a bonus for sure. I hated that I had to be a hired gun who took cases I didn't really want, but at the same time, the kids' private school was not cheap, and both of them wanted to go to Harvard. I knew they both were smart enough to do just that, so I had to put as much money away as possible. My multi-million dollar settlement a few years back would only go so far in today's world.

"So what time can I come back?" he asked me coolly.

I regarded him, not wanting for him to come back at all, yet also feeling something pulling me into this case against my better judgment.

"Come back at 4 o'clock. I can only give you an hour though. After that, I have to head home." I actually had planned on heading home even earlier than 4 o'clock that day, but I supposed I could make some time out for this guy. "I have to warn you though, I'm leaning against taking your case. I just don't want to deal with the publicity, for one thing, but also, I've read the newspaper article about you, and I just don't like to sign up misogynists." I was raised by a woman who attracted nothing but violent misogynists, so I, as a rule, wanted nothing to do with misogynistic men when they showed up in my office wanting me to represent them.

"I assure you I am not a misogynist. No matter what the paper says about me, I assure you I'm not a misogynist. I respect women very much. I will tell you upfront, however, I am into the lifestyle. The alternative lifestyle."

"By lifestyle, I assume you mean you're into BDSM, right?"

"Yes, you are correct about that. I wanted to tell you this right up front because that's a part of my story. I would never intentionally kill my wife. I loved her very much. She and I had a very passionate relationship but it was also based upon mutual respect." When he said that, he had a sad look in his eye, and I almost believed him. It was the first time I'd seen some kind of emotion in his eyes and that encouraged me a bit.

"Okay. I'll see you in a few hours. In the meantime, I have to get prepared for my deposition, so I'm sorry, but I really have to get going."

"Of course. I understand. You have a life and it was rude to drop in on you like this. So thank you for at least being willing to hear my story. I'll see you soon."

At that, he left. And I felt I could breathe. I shook my head, wondering what the hell I was doing. This guy freaked me out, more than anybody had in a long time. And yet I was considering taking him on as a client. What was my problem?

I didn't know what my problem was. I only knew I was

somehow getting involved with a situation I didn't want to get involved with. And yet I had a feeling that when all was said and done, he would be my client.

I just hoped I didn't live to regret that. Although I knew I would.

## Chapter Two

I GOT BACK from my deposition, and found that Silas was waiting for me once again. This time, he didn't stare at me, but, rather, he actually smiled a little bit. I swallowed hard. "Mr. Porter, come into my office, and I need to get your side of the story."

"Of course." He followed me into my office, and we both sat down while I closed the door behind him.

I got a yellow pad of paper and a pen and started to write. "Okay, here's what I read in the paper. I read your wife was chained to a wall when a fire swept through your dungeon. As I understand it, from reading the newspaper, your dungeon is a structure you have behind your swimming pool. It was formerly used as servant's quarters, from what you told the police, but you currently are using it as your dungeon. Is that correct?"

He nodded. "Yes, that is correct."

"The way she died is partly why I don't want to take this case. I just can't imagine being in her position. Being helpless and not able to do anything and seeing a fire sweep through. I'm sure she died in agony." I had Public Defender cases where I represented drug dealers accused of burning people to death. Those were some of the worst cases I'd ever encountered. Of course, those were also cases I ended up pleading out. I had a feeling I would have to try this case, assuming I took it. Which meant I would get into all the painful details of what happened.

"I assure you my wife did not burn to death. She was dead before the fire swept through the dungeon."

"What do you mean?" If she was dead before the fire got to her, that would be better facts for me. Marginally better, but better nonetheless. "Are you telling me something else killed her besides the fire?"

"Yes, that's what I'm telling you. There was a preliminary autopsy done on the body. However, since my wife's body was severely burned, as she ended up just ashes and bones, there wasn't much that could be ascertained about how she died. You'll find out all of this when you get the file. To tell you the truth, I don't know how my wife died. I have no idea."

I sighed. "Okay, please explain what you mean. Are you saying that –"

"I'm telling you my wife and I were being intimate, and, I will admit, we typically do things that skirt the line of what is safe and what's not. I can also tell you we never crossed that line and never came close to it. For instance, we were involved with body bag bondage. Are you aware of that term?"

"I am." I had a little bit of knowledge about BDSM because I'd once taken a case where a child was in the house when his mother and her boyfriend were involved in the practice. The child's actual father was suing for custody, because he didn't want his son exposed to that in the home. I had to do as much research as possible on the lifestyle for that case so I felt reasonably informed.

I knew body bag bondage involved putting one's partner into a body bag and suffocating them to the point that they would almost pass out. This act apparently gives the participants some kind of a high. Apparently, whenever you restricted your air in that way, you get lightheaded, which induces mild euphoria. Men often strangled themselves with a belt while they masturbated, and this practice was called auto-erotic asphyxiation. Sometimes they ended up accidentally killing themselves when they did that. Allegedly, the famous actor David Carradine, of *Kung Fu* fame, and Michael Hutchence, the lead singer of INXS, died that way.

"Well, if you're familiar with the concept of body bag bondage, then you know about the level my wife and I went to when we would play. In this case, I had her chained to a wall. That was something we did often. And we were intimate that way." He paused. "She asked me to put a plastic bag over her head, which I often do. I know how long I can do that before it gets dangerous. I timed it perfectly, the way I always have, but, when I took the plastic bag off her head, she was dead."

I made notes as he spoke. "So this was something you two did habitually and it was never a problem before?"

"Right. So I didn't know how she died. I am trained in CPR of course. That was mandatory for both Ava and me - we both had to know how to revive one another if the time came. So I unchained her and was going to perform CPR, but then I saw she completely stopped breathing and I found no pulse. She was dead. I had no idea how. But I wanted to try to revive her anyway, so I went to get the key to the lock for her handcuff. The fire suddenly came out of nowhere and swept through our dungeon. It was a conflagration. I had no idea how it got to be so much of a wildfire in such a short period of time. I don't know where it came from."

"That's the reason why you were charged with her murder - it sounds like there was some kind of accelerant in the fire. Is that what happened?"

He nodded silently. I could see pain in his expression, and the fact he had emotion behind those light eyes made me feel slightly more comfortable with him.

"Yes. That's why I was charged with her murder. Yes, when the investigators came to the house, they found an accelerant. I was barely able to get out of the dungeon myself. I was barely able to outrun the fire. It was that swift. I'm lucky to be alive. But yes, the investigators decided my dungeon burned down because of arson. Because Ava was chained to a wall at the time, they just assumed I burned down my own dungeon while entrapping her because I wanted to kill her. That her parents were pushing the police to charge me with her murder did not help matters any. They've always hated me. They've never thought I was good enough for their daughter. They didn't even know about our lifestyle - they just didn't like me because I came from nothing. I think they wanted her to marry somebody whose last name was Vanderbilt or Carnegie or something along those lines. So when Ava died in such a way, they were pressuring the police to make an arrest. And that's how I got arrested."

I made a note about this. I would have to talk to Ava's parents and find out what the real story was. I needed to find out if it was true that they just didn't like him because he grew up poor. I knew he was telling the truth when he said he didn't grow up wealthy. I had read in the paper that his mother worked as a waitress and an office cleaner and his father worked at Walmart and as a cook. Of course, I wouldn't take him at his word that the only reason why Ava's parents hated him was because he wasn't "good enough" for her. It was entirely possible the newspaper article was true – Silas might've been a wife abuser. I would have to get to the bottom of that before I made a decision or judgment on this case.

For the moment, however, I would have to take him at his word. If he told me the only reason Ava's parents hated him was because he grew up poor, then I would just have to take that as gospel until I found out differently.

"Okay, so Ava's parents were pushing for you to be arrested for her murder."

"Yes. But it wasn't a murder. I still don't know how she died. I have no clue. We were doing our usual playing, and as far as I know, she wasn't even sick." He shook his head. "It was as if she had a heart attack, a massive heart attack, and died. However, she was only 32 years old. And, as far as I know, she did not have a heart problem."

"Are you sure about that? Are you sure she didn't have a heart problem?"

He shifted uncomfortably in his seat. "No, I'm not sure about that." He blinked a few times. "I do know my wife was seeing a doctor at the time she died, however, as far as I know, there was nothing wrong with her."

"What do you mean, as far as you know, there was nothing wrong with her?" I wondered how much Silas really knew about his wife. It was entirely possible she had a heart problem but didn't tell him about it. After all, if she enjoyed participating in bondage games with Silas, maybe she didn't want to tell him she had a heart issue - maybe she figured if she told him about her heart issue, he wouldn't play those games with her. That would be a reason for her to hide any kind of health issues from him.

"Exactly what I said. I don't believe she had any health issues. However, I'm not positive about that. I would always ask her if there were health issues I needed to know about and she always told me she was fine and healthy." He shook his head. "That said, I suspected maybe there was something wrong with her. I never saw any prescriptions around the house. But when I got back from Europe, I noticed she had lost a lot of weight and seemed very tired and fatigued. I guess it's possible she was suffering from some kind of heart issue, or some other kind of undisclosed health issue, and that's what killed her."

"But you never saw any prescriptions, correct?"

"That is correct."

I bounced my pen up and down on the page, as I thought about what he was telling me. "Did you travel with her?"

"I used to. I used to travel with her all the time. As you probably know, I travel quite a bit for my work. In fact, I was overseas in Europe for six months. I had just returned when this happened. From Europe that is. And she did not go with me."

"She didn't go with you? So I guess it's possible she was suffering from some kind of health issues and you might not have known about it because you were overseas."

"That is definitely a possibility." He clenched his jaw. Tapped his fingers on the desk. "I suppose you could get her medical records, and find out if there was anything wrong with her. There must've been something. There had to have been some reason why she died the way she did. All I can tell you is she was dead before the fire swept in and I did not do anything to bring about her death."

I knew the prosecutors probably were aware that Silas and Ava were involved in BDSM. And, because of that, they probably reasonably thought maybe Ava died during some kind of hard-core playing, unless they just assumed Silas had set the fire in his own home to kill his wife.

"Now, let's get back to what the newspapers say about your relationship with Ava. It indicated you were abusive with her. Is that true?"

He straightened up in his chair and glared at me. "I told you that was not true. I told you that earlier. In no way, shape or form was I abusive to her. Some people don't understand alternative lifestyles – they think people involved in these lifestyles are abusive to one another. Or, especially, the man is abusive to the woman because the woman likes to be beaten, or whipped, or degraded. By the way, our relationship did not involve any of those things. I did not whip her, I did not beat her, and I did not degrade her. I did not humiliate her. We were more into bondage than anything else. The body bags, the chains, the feeling of latex. She enjoyed being confined. I sometimes put her into a small box, the size of a coffin. I would put her in there for a very set period of time. Just like I would put her into a body bag for a very set period of time. I knew my limitations and knew hers as well. And I've never come close to the point where I would have accidentally killed her. You have to trust me on this. So when she died, there was nothing I did that brought it about."

"You do know I'm going to be speaking with her friends, and her parents, and people who were aware of her situation with you. I need to know from you what kind of story I'm going to hear from them. What kind of words am I going to hear from her friends and family and people whom she held dear?"

"Her parents will tell you I was abusive to her. That's what they told the newspaper. But you have to understand, they have their own agenda. They want to see me fry. They're convinced I murdered my wife and did it in cold blood. There are a variety of reasons why they are so convinced about that. So, fair warning, that's the kind of story you'll get from them. As for her friends, I don't know what kind of story they'll give you. I don't know what Ava told them about her relationship with me. I don't think they believed I was abusive to her, however. They have no reason to believe that."

"But her parents have a reason to believe that? Why would they have reason to believe that but her friends don't?"

"Because they have an agenda." He rolled his eyes. He tapped his fingers on the desk and took a deep breath. "She had bruises."

I made a note of this. "She had bruises? But you told me you didn't beat her. So why would she have bruises?"

"I didn't beat her. And that's the truth. However, other people beat her."

"What's that supposed to mean?"

Silas made a steeple with his hands. "I allowed my wife to stray. She had very singular desires and fantasies, and I couldn't fulfill them. I had a problem with beating and whipping her, but she needed that in her life, so I allowed her to see people who would do that for her. And she allowed me to see other people as well."

"So you had an open relationship." It wasn't a question on my part. It was a statement.

"Yes. We definitely had an open relationship. That's why

she had bruises on her arms. But her parents did not understand that, and there was no way Ava would tell them the truth. She would never tell them she was into this lifestyle. Her parents would never understand such a thing. Most people would never understand such a thing. So, the upshot is, her parents just assumed I was beating her, and had no idea her beatings were consensual and were not from me."

I leaned back in my chair. His story was not sitting well with me. There were just too many holes in it. "You told me when you walked in that the only reason her parents hated you was because you came from a poor background. But now you're telling me her parents had good reason to suspect you were beating on her, their daughter. Wouldn't that be a better reason for them to hate you then the fact you were poor at one time?"

"Yes. I agree. But they hated me long before they ever saw the bruises on her. I guess it's possible they suspected our relationship was unconventional, right from the start. I don't know. All I know is that they've never accepted me, right from the very beginning."

"And why didn't Ava set her parents straight? Why didn't she tell them you weren't beating her? Why didn't she try to hide her bruises from them if she didn't know what to say to them?" That was another niggling fact rolling around in my brain. Ava had to know her parents hated Silas, so why throw fuel on the fire? Why allow them to believe he was physically abusing her?

"Ava did not deliberately let her parents see she had bruises on her arms. She covered up her arms whenever she went to visit them. However, she had the misfortune to have her parents visit her unexpectedly one day at our home. She was wearing short sleeves and they saw them. She told me she told them she fell down during the night when she was sleep-walking but said they didn't seem to believe her. They asked her outright if I was beating her. She denied it, but they didn't appear to believe her." He looked away. "They would never give me the benefit of the doubt."

I studied him. I was not at all sure if I could or should believe him. In fact, I was inclined not to believe him. I was naturally skeptical anyhow when it came to my clients. I had to be. When you are a criminal defense attorney, you had to go into your cases assuming your client is lying to you. You had to be cynical in this job.

I decided to briefly change the subject because I was really curious about one thing. "Why did you single me out for this job?"

"I looked into your background. It seems like you've won a lot of your cases. That in and of itself is quite unusual. It seems like you have the special touch for picking the right jury that will exonerate your clients. And you have quite the impressive list of clients. There's no other reason why I would choose you."

I had to admit he was making some kind of sense, but that still didn't answer the question I had about that. He was so adamant about my representing him. The way he sounded when he first came into my office was that he would hound me until I said yes.

I narrowed my eyes. Why was there a question in my mind about why he was so keen to have me represent him? Why did I think there was more to the story? As I looked at him, with those light eyes that were now staring at me again, with no emotion behind them, I felt the earlier chill up and down my spine.

"I'll be honest with you, I don't feel you're telling me the entire truth. I think there's more to why you want me to represent you. I'm getting a sick feeling in my gut and my gut is rarely wrong. As you noted earlier, I am very good with picking a jury, because I go with my gut when it comes to choosing the right panel. I can usually tell if people are lying. And I think you are lying right now. So please tell me the real reason why you want me to represent you so much. And know this – what you don't tell me, I will find out on my own. Sooner or later, I will find out. So you might as well just come out with it."

He studied me, silently looking at me from across the desk. I couldn't tell what he was thinking and that unnerved me. "Are you going to take my case?"

"Are you going to answer my question?"

"I already did."

"Not honestly."

"Perhaps you think my answer wasn't honest. I can't help that. Now are you going to take my case?"

I decided to test him. "My fee is $1000 per hour. I demand a retainer of $100,000 upfront." My actual fee was normally only $400 per hour and I imagined this guy knew this. If he did his homework on me, he would know what I usually charge. I was just testing him to see exactly how much he wanted me to represent him. Would he just allow me to name my price like that? Or would he call me on it? If he really wanted me to represent him, desperately wanted me to represent him, he would pay my fee without question. After all, he clearly could afford it. Writing a check for $100,000 would be nothing to him. It would be like me writing somebody a check for $100. However, with him being a businessman, I was sure he would object to being price-gouged, which was exactly what I was trying to do.

I saw in his eyes he understood what I was doing, but he calmly brought out a checkbook. "Do I make it out to you? Or do I make it out to your firm?"

I cleared my throat. "You may make it out to our firm." I was still an associate, although I was in talks with Harper to make me a full partner. That decision would come soon, maybe within the next few days. Most of this fee, of course, would go into my trust fund. That's the way it always had to be – whenever you received a retainer from your client, you had to put all of that money into a trust fund, and then, as you did the work, you could withdraw money from the trust fund to put into your operating account. Of course, at the rate of $1000 per hour, I would definitely go through his retainer in no time.

I held my breath as I saw him writing out a check. "Here's my check for $200,000," he said. "That will get you through about 200 hours worth of work. I understand I'm going to probably have to replenish this, as this case will be tangled, to say the very least. I also understand you'll have investigators, paralegals and researchers working on my case. We'll have to go over how much their time is worth as well."

I reached into my drawer and brought out a contract. "I do have a paralegal, her name is Heather. For her work, I bill at the rate of $200 per hour. I have investigators. They, too, bill at the rate of $200 per hour." Ordinarily, I would bill at the rate of $100 per hour for Heather, and that same rate for the investigators, who were Tom Garrett, Nick Savante and Jack O'Brien, who weren't just my investigators but were also my friends. They did a very good, thorough job. I also had Anna, our hacker. She could get records I couldn't get through more legitimate means. For her services, I also usually billed $100 per hour. However, for this case, I would bill all of their services at $200 per hour. This guy apparently was willing to pay any amount, so I might as well put a premium on everybody's work.

He looked over the contract thoroughly and signed it. "So you'll start getting to work immediately?"

I nodded and said nothing. I was surprised he was so willing to pay such a higher dollar amount for my services. He didn't question it. Didn't even blink. I was charging him as much as a white-shoe firm would charge and I was far from being a white-shoe lawyer. Granted, any amount of money he would pay me would be a drop in the bucket for him, but still.

I crossed my arms in front of me and wondered what his game was. "As I told you before, I'm going to find out anything you're not telling me. So if there's something I need to know about why you want me so badly to represent you, you need to come clean about it right now."

He simply put his checkbook back in his jacket pocket and stood up. "I can certainly visit you anytime you need me to speak with you. As you might imagine, as a condition of my bail, I cannot leave the country. In fact, I cannot leave the jurisdiction. So, I have assigned my international travel to my deputy. That means I will be at your disposal. I will be in my office as I plan on keeping a full work schedule. But I will make any time you need."

"Okay. I appreciate that."

He tapped his fingers on my desk again. "Is there anything more you need from me right now?"

"At the moment, no. Although I'm sure that once I start getting into the investigation of this case, I'll have to speak with you." I had a feeling that when I spoke with her parents and her friends, I would get a very different picture about Silas' relationship with Ava.

He stood up. "Very well then," he said. He gave me his business card. "I know I filled out a client intake sheet, however, I still want you to have this. I need for you to call me anytime of the day or night if you need to speak with me. I have nothing to hide. I hope you know that."

As he walked away, I wondered about that. Briefly. I wondered if it was true he had nothing to hide. My gut was telling me he had a lot to hide.

And my gut was never wrong.

## Chapter Three

THAT NIGHT, I decided to have a small dinner party. I invited both Harper and Tammy over to share a meal with me and the kids. After dinner, I would speak with both of them about my becoming a partner. That was the reason why I wanted Tammy around as well. Obviously, since she was an equal partner with Harper, she would have to be okay with bringing me on as another partner. I also wanted to speak with both of them about the situation with Silas. I knew Tammy probably knew his story. In fact, she had come into my office briefly and asked me about it after he left.

I would pick both of their brains about it and ask them what they thought.

I got home and saw my kids waiting there for me, with Gretchen, the neighborhood girl who watched them after school. Things were still tense between me and the kids, for different reasons, but they were gradually getting better. Amelia and I had to come to terms with the fact I wasn't her biological father, so things had been weird between us for the past several months. As for Nate, he was gradually starting to hate me less each day. After the divorce, he refused, for months, to speak to me. For some odd reason, he adored his mother, even though she was a no-account witch who abandoned the family when Amelia was possibly dying of cancer, taking up with another man and pretending the kids didn't exist.

Then, after all was said and done, she revealed to Amelia that her biological father was somebody else - my own half-brother, Jake Brillis, as it turned out. She was apparently screwing him while married to me, which was fine, once I thought about it - after all, her affair produced Amelia, and since I couldn't picture my life without my young daughter, I really had to mentally tip my hat to both Sarah and her lover. What pissed me off was that Sarah told Amelia about the paternity issue, all because she wanted money - Sarah and her current lover, Baron Wicker, hatched up a scheme to falsify DNA evidence that showed Baron was Amelia's dad. Apparently, Baron, a rich bastard, wanted to be an even richer bastard and needed an heir before he could collect on a coming inheritance from his terminally-ill grandmother. I managed to catch them in the act, with the help of Nick, my best friend and investigator, who uncovered the scheme. I threatened Sarah with criminal prosecution and a lawsuit, which made her back down.

"Hey, Dad," Amelia said when I came through the door. She motioned over to Nate, who looked visibly shaken. "Nate's kinda freaked out right now. Guess I don't blame him, after what happened at his school today."

Nate was 10 years old and in the fifth grade, while Amelia was 8 and in the third grade. They both were in a private school, although they went to separate ones. "What happened at his school?" I asked Amelia.

She said nothing but just gestured over to him. "Ask him," she said. "Not my story to tell."

I looked over at my sullen son, who just shrugged his shoulders. "Not a big deal. Some clown brought a gun into school. Guess he was mad at one of his teachers."

I sighed. I hated that the kids had to worry about such things as weapons being brought into school. I never did when I was their age. The Columbine massacre happened when I was 16 and in the 11th Grade. Before that, school shootings were almost unheard of. Since then, they were becoming routine. Too routine for my money. "So, what happened? They lock everything down?"

"Sure," Nate said nonchalantly. "They locked everything down then the cops came and took him away. Just another day at my richie-rich private school, Dad. Turns out kids who got money are just as screwed up as the ones who don't."

I never imagined there would come a day when I would be concerned that one or both of my kids weren't safe at their schools, but that day had finally come. Not that I could do anything about it. I could have them home-schooled if I was that worried about the two of them getting shot at their school, but I knew that, in the end, the odds were astronomically against something like that happening, so I would stay with the status quo. "You need to talk about that, buddy?" I asked him. "It had to be scary for you to see that kind of thing."

He shook his head. "No, Dad, I don't. I'm okay. I don't think that kid was actually going to shoot somebody. I heard the gun wasn't even loaded." He shrugged again. "I guess his parents are splitting up and he's having a hard time with it. They brought in a school counselor and everything to come and talk to us if we were scared and stuff. I wasn't scared, so I didn't talk to the counselor. I mean, Dad, you see guys with guns all the time. If you're not scared of guys with guns, I'm not scared, either."

I cleared my throat. I was still trying to get under the layers with Nate - the defensive layers. He was a mysterious kid in a lot of ways. He never could confess how he was really feeling about any given situation, it seemed. Just like when he clammed up when Sarah and I got divorced, instead of screaming or crying or even just talking about his feelings, he dealt with all problems in that same way - shrugging his shoulders and changing the subject. Acting like nothing mattered. Of course, things mattered to him, but it was hard getting him to admit that.

"Nate," I said, "don't snow me about this. A kid brought a gun into your school. That's serious business. I'm going to have to talk to your school administrators about what kind of safety measures they're going to take to make sure this doesn't happen again, that goes without saying, but, Nate, you have to talk to me about how you really feel." I was his age once, of course, and if some goofball brought a gun into school, I would've been freaked out, to say the least. Of course, when I was his age, I was dealing with my own problems - a mother with a revolving door of men and a stepfather physically abusing me on a regular basis, which led me to killing him in his sleep when I was just 15. I certainly didn't have the privileged life Nate had, that was for sure, yet, even at my hard-scrabble school, nobody actually brought a gun, let alone brandished it.

"Dad, really, it's no big deal," he said. "I don't know why you have to make it seem like it's some huge prob. It's not. The kid got taken away by the cops, the other kids all said he's not coming back, and now I guess we'll have metal detectors and stuff and we're all going to have clear backpacks. I also heard we'll get some kind of rent-a-cop to watch over us, but I think that's just stupid." He shook his head. "Why don't they just wrap us all in bubble wrap and call it a day?"

If only wrapping my kids in bubble wrap would protect them…"Okay. Well, if you need somebody to talk to, I'm the only game in town, kiddo. In the meantime, I got Harper and Tammy coming over for dinner, and I need your guys' help in getting dinner ready."

We went into the kitchen. The kids got busy chopping onions and peppers for our chili, while I opened up cans of tomatoes. After Amelia was done with her pepper, I put her to work in making the cornbread mix, which was something she loved doing. I secretly thought Amelia was destined to become a chef one day because she really had quite an affinity for cooking. At the age of 8, she didn't just have scrambled eggs in her repertoire, but also chicken alfredo pasta, lasagna and chicken pot pie. She loved watching cooking shows on TV and there was more than one occasion when she looked up the recipes she saw the celebrity chef making and tried to make it herself.

As I browned the meat and threw the onions, peppers and tomatoes into the skillet, I talked to the kids. "Are you sure you don't mind Harper and Tammy coming over tonight?" I asked both of the kids.

"Dad," Amelia said. "Of course I want them to come over. Don't be silly. I mean, I'm freaked out, but I'll be okay. I promise I'll be okay." She motioned to Nate. "I think he's okay with it, too."

"Are you, kiddo?" I asked him.

He shrugged. "Sure, Dad," he said with a shrug.

The kids and I made the chili, and then I heard the doorbell ring. I saw both Tammy and Harper on the other side of the door. I opened up, they came in. "Look at us," Tammy said. "We just happened to arrive at the exact same time."

"That is unusual." After all, Harper was usually running late. But apparently not this evening. It was right at 7 o'clock, which was the time I asked them to come over.

We had dinner and I sent the kids into the room to go do homework and do whatever they wanted to do once their homework was finished. That was their usual routine. The kids were allowed their private time, to do whatever they wanted to do, as long as they got their homework done. I then checked to make sure their homework was finished before they could play video games or read or watch television or whatever kids do these days. I really didn't need to check on their homework – both kids were honor roll students. Yet I knew how I was when I was growing up. I was always trying to get out of doing homework. I figured that was an age-old problem, really.

Is that what kids always do? Try to get one over on their parents?

The kids were upstairs and Tammy and Harper I went out into the sunroom to talk about the possibility of my becoming a partner. I had brought in a lot of business in the time I had been with them, and they considered me a valuable member of our team. There was a time when I was afraid I would go to prison for the rest of my life, as I had been accused of killing my father. Thank God that time had passed.

"Okay," Harper began. "We need to go over the terms for your partnership."

"Yeah, we'll talk about that," Tammy said to Harper and then she turned to me. "I know that's what you wanted to talk about. But I was curious about Silas Porter. I read about him in the paper. I read about what he did. Will he be your client?"

I took a deep breath. I had signed Silas on, against my own better judgment, but I still wasn't entirely clear I wanted to enter an appearance on his behalf. There was a part of me that still wanted to back out of the contract and pay whatever kind of damages I would have to pay to get out of it. I got into that contract in haste, really, when I thought about it. What was I doing, getting involved with the guy who possibly murdered his wife in cold blood and probably was an abusive person as well? He told me, of course, he wasn't, but I just knew that when I spoke with the people who were Ava's friends and family, I would get a different story, one that was not so sugarcoated and pretty as what he gave me. That was usually the case. In this case, I was sure of it. This guy seemed like somebody hiding a lot.

"Yeah. He's my client as of now. Why do you ask that question?"

Tammy shrugged. "I just didn't think that was the kind of thing you would want to get involved with. I mean, let's face facts. I've been paying attention to this case, and it seems like your client has a lot of problems. Not that that's a big deal. Of course not. You guys have dealt with some pretty hardened criminals in your careers. I just didn't think a guy like Silas is somebody you'd want to take on as a client."

"Why is that?"

"Well, I know you're very sensitive about people who abuse women. Because of what happened to your mother. I know you get especially squeamish when the guy has money and power. So it seems like it's a perfect storm with this guy as far as the things you try to avoid. I'm just surprised you would take these issues on."

"Well –" I opened my mouth but I really didn't know what to say. Granted, Silas insisted to me that his relationship with Ava was not abusive. But it made me suspicious that she had those bruises on her body.

"Well, what?" Harper asked me. "I agree with Tammy. I think you're playing with fire here. The media has already found out you're going to represent him and they've already started calling the office. Pearl's been talking to them, but you're going to have a lot of messages to return in the morning. You'll have to respond to these media inquiries. Silas is the kind of person who's going to want you to."

Ordinarily, I tried never to speak about my clients to anybody. It was always my policy never to comment on an open investigation or an open case. That was always the best way to do it. But, at the same time, I knew Silas would want to get his side of the story out. His publicist would give his story but I had a feeling he wanted me also put out a statement. And, at the moment, I had no idea about the kind of statement I would put out. I still didn't know what was going on in this case. I had my suspicions, but I wanted to get more into it before I talked to anybody about it, and that included the media.

"How do you know so much about Silas? How do you know he'll be the kind of person who will want me to speak with the media about his case?"

"Because it's obvious. The stories coming out about him are horrible. You have to read them. I know you probably read at least one of the stories, but you should read some of the other ones. These stories are really portraying him as being a piece of work. And did you know he was in a mental hospital?"

I narrowed my eyes. For some odd reason, the fact that Silas had been in a mental hospital concerned me. I guess it was because he had such a demeanor when I met him. A cold, calculating demeanor. It was as if I was in the midst of a serial killer. That was the kind of feeling I got. So to find out he had some kind of mental issues did not sit well with me. To say the very least. "Do you know why he was in the mental hospital?"

Tammy shrugged. "It's just what I've been hearing. It's not been reported yet in the paper, or in the media in general, because that's the kind of thing you have to find out for sure or else somebody can sue you for libel. And, from my media contacts, they tell me they have not yet been able to verify that fact. I've heard it off the record."

"Why are you so interested in this case already? I mean, Silas just came into my office today. You had time to do all this research already?"

Tammy looked embarrassed. A little ashamed. "Well, no. Actually, Pearl told me earlier on, actually yesterday, that Silas had called for you. You were in court and then you went home. So you didn't even know about it. But when I found out he had called to make an appointment with you, I started looking into it. I'm sorry, I'm just looking out for you. I know how you get. And I know what you've been through. Plus, I remembered reading the paper about this case and I wanted to find out about him before you decided to take him on as a client. I didn't know he would come back into the office so soon. I wanted to talk to you about it before you were going to sign a contract for representation with him. I guess I didn't get to you soon enough and I regret that. Very sorry about that."

"It's okay," I assured her. "Thank you for looking out for me." I would have to get information about when and where he allegedly went into the mental hospital.

"Are you sure it was a mental hospital? Maybe it was a

rehab facility or something of the sort. A lot of guys in high stress positions end up having some kind of drug problem because they have to work so much. Using cocaine, meth and speed is not necessarily unheard of in high-powered professions. Maybe that was all it was."

Then again, I knew Harper was in the hospital several years back. She was having a manic episode and didn't even know at that time that she was bipolar. She just figured she was depressed because she'd never before had a manic episode. I knew that being in a mental hospital does not necessarily mean that one was crazy, but, rather, sometimes it just meant meds needed to be adjusted. That was how it was in Harper's case.

Tammy just nodded. I knew she was thinking the same thing I was – I would have to find out exactly what led Silas into a mental hospital. She knew what kind of issues Harper had, so I knew she wanted to be sensitive and not try to imply Silas was insane or something like that. "I just wanted you to know about that. That's all. Although I'm sure you would have found out about it sooner or later in your research on the guy."

"That's true. It definitely would come up." Since Silas signed a release for medical records, I knew that finding out what Silas' issue was wouldn't be a problem. "What else have you heard? I admit, I haven't really gotten too far into this case. I'm going to order the file tomorrow. I know I should have figured out what kind of person he was before I signed him up, and I just think it's very strange he wanted me to represent him so much. He was very adamant he wanted only me to represent him. Do you think that's odd?"

Harper shook her head. "No, I don't have that thought at all. You're an attorney with a stellar reputation and you've won most of your cases. I sure as hell would want you on my side if I was charged with a crime."

"That's what he said. I just think there's more to it, though. That's all. I suppose it will come out in time. I just hope it doesn't come out too late."

Harper decided to change the subject. "In the meantime, we discussed making you partner. Tammy and I had some partnership papers drawn up for you to look over and sign. It's pretty standard. We'll all be equal partners – one-third, one-third, one-third. I know you and I have talked about it as well and I know you're interested in doing this. So let's just get this over with and we can have a glass of champagne. Or, rather, the two of you can have a glass of champagne mand I'll stick to my sparkling grape juice."

I looked over the partnership papers and then signed them. We all raised a glass. It was good to be a partner. After what I went through with being under suspicion for the murder of my father, and everything that dug up for me, it felt good to have something positive finally happen.

Life was good at the moment. I just hoped that didn't change.

## Chapter Four

THE NEXT DAY, I answered some reporter's questions and made a brief statement to the press, at Silas' blessing, and I made a motion to the court for me to inspect the crime scene. Silas had described to me what he called his dungeon, but I wanted to see it for myself. The judge had signed the order for me, so I was allowed to go over to his home and take a look at the place where Ava died.

I also had ordered the file, and it had come in. I needed to find out more information about him, and I also needed to find out more details on what had actually happened when Ava had passed away. I also had Pearl prepare a subpoena for Ava's medical records. I just had a feeling there was something wrong with her health that Silas didn't know about. And if that was the case, I would feel better about taking Silas on as a client. After all, if Ava was seriously ill, that would mean Silas' story was possibly true. Maybe she had an undisclosed heart issue, and what she was doing with Silas taxed her so much that her heart gave out. Or maybe there was another reason why. I didn't know.

I got to the house. It was one of those 10,000 square-foot homes nestled in the heart of Hallbrook, an exclusive enclave in Leawood, Kansas. This was a neighborhood where Joe Montana once lived, when he played quarterback for the Chiefs, along with CEOs and captains of industry.

Silas met me at the home, along with Ally and a police officer, and he led us around to the back patio. I needed to take a look at the burned-out dungeon, and then would take a look inside the house. I wanted to see if there were any kind of clues inside the house that would've told me that perhaps things were not as Silas had described them.

"There's not much to see, I'm afraid," Silas said as I followed him through his backyard. "At least, there's not much to see of our dungeon."

The backyard consisted of an in-ground swimming pool surrounded by statues and a structure that was once probably at least a 1,000 square foot home. It appeared to be either a guest house or servant's quarters. According to the pictures Silas showed me, it was a smaller version of the main house. At the moment, however, it was nothing but a pile of rubble. Investigators had left it the way it was, because it was considered to be a crime scene.

As I looked at the pile of rubble, I shuddered. All that was standing was a brick wall with a pair of handcuffs attached. Other than that, however, that structure was nothing but ashes.

"This is where they found her," Silas said, pointing to the handcuffs attached to the brick wall. "There wasn't much left of her, I'm afraid."

I took out the file and looked at the picture of the body. Silas was correct about that – there wasn't much left of his wife. Her body was little more than a pile of ashes and bones. In the picture, I could also see her two hands were still intact and bound in the handcuffs.

As I walked and poked along the rubble, being careful not to disturb anything, because I knew this was still a crime scene, I asked questions about what this dungeon contained.

"It was outfitted with the usual implements. A St. Andrew's Cross, handcuffs, a box where I enclosed her, latex suits, body bags, and there was also a whipping altar where I bent down while she beat me."

This was a different piece of information. "Are you saying you would occasionally be submissive to her?"

"Of course. Occasionally she was dominant. Mainly, I was dominant. But, as I said, I didn't beat her or whip her. She needed that but didn't get it from me."

I felt satisfied that there was not much more I could really glean from looking at this charred remains of a dungeon, so I went inside the main house. Fortunately for Silas, the main house was not touched by the flames. That was because the dungeon was on the other side of the pool. Once the flames reached the concrete, they would've died out. The upshot was that the dungeon was burned to the ground but the actual house was completely intact.

I walked in the house and looked around. It was modern, with gleaming marble floors and a skylight in the ceiling that was a good 20 feet above my head. I looked through the game room, the living room, the dining room, the master bedroom and the seven other bedrooms. I didn't know what I was looking for, but I wanted to see if I could find any clues about Ava's health.

I went through all six of the bathrooms, looking for some prescriptions. I saw none. I walked into the master bedroom where I saw a closet with various outfits that looked like what a woman would wear during sex play - leather bustiers, high heels, leather panties, leather catsuits and bodysuits, leather pants and skirts, and leather hats. The presence of these outfits validated Silas's story about how he and Ava engaged in sex play, which was significant to me. That told me that there was, indeed, a legitimate reason for Ava being chained to that wall when fire swept in. It also told me that, on this point at least, Silas wasn't lying.

I walked through the rest of the house and didn't see anything amiss. Silas accompanied me, as did a member of the Police Department who had met me at the house, as this was still a crime scene, so the cop was there to make sure I didn't defile the evidence in some way. Also there was a prosecutor, Ally Hughes. She trailed me through the house, along with the police officer.

"I don't know what I'm looking for," I admitted. Then I went into another bathroom, looking for more prescriptions, and I came up on a few, but they were made out to my client, not to Ava. One of the prescriptions was for Geodon, which I knew was a drug prescribed for people who had mood disorders. I knew this because I had some experience in the past with clients who suffered from bi-polar disorder, and this was a common drug prescribed for this. I also saw he was prescribed Prozac.

I looked at Silas standing in the door. I couldn't read his expression, but it looked like he was annoyed I was getting into his personal things. "So you know my secret."

"Having bipolar disorder is nothing to be ashamed of and I'm glad to see you are actually taking medicine for it." I always saw meds that people take for mood disorders as being no different than meds one takes for diabetes or high blood pressure or any other kind of health issue. You wouldn't be stigmatized for taking insulin, so why would you be stigmatized for taking Prozac?

He nodded. "I'll admit I wasn't always taking medicine for my issues. There were many years when I was living with undiagnosed bi-polar disorder and I wasn't dealing with it very well. I had severe problems with alcohol and you will find out I also had issues with anger. I didn't tell you about my bi-polar disorder because I didn't want you to judge me."

He had problems with anger? This was just now coming out? "Did these problems with anger cause you to be abusive to Ava or any other person along the way?" I wondered if he was lying to me about what he was saying earlier about how he could never lay a hand on his wife. Maybe he caused the bruises on her arms after all.

I looked around and saw Ally was standing to the side. I hoped she didn't hear anything being said. "You're going to have to talk to me about this later. At the moment, however, I'm going to take you at your word - what you told me earlier." I looked at him meaningful with a look that said that we couldn't talk about this subject at the moment and he seemed to understand.

"Of course."

I inspected the rest of the house, but there wasn't anything else that gave me any kind of pause. "Okay. I guess it's time for me to leave. You want to follow me to my office so we can talk about things?" Now that I had the file in hand, I had the basis to ask him more meaningful questions.

"I'll follow you over."

I shook hands with the prosecutor and the officer and went to my car. Silas got into his own Tesla and he followed me to my office, where I got right down to asking him questions. "Now, you told me briefly at the house you had anger problems. Can you just tell me what kind of problems you were having?"

He steepled his hands, and looked down at my desk. "You have to understand that for many years, I was living with bipolar disorder, and I had no idea. That was probably the reason why I became successful. See, I was able to work around the clock when I was experiencing periods of mania. And I had such great insight. I felt like I was using all of my brain, and could see my way around problems I could never figure out before. And I took a lot of chances. I gambled a lot. Not just playing the stock market, and things like that, but also took a lot of chances with the business when I started it up. Because of my great insight, most of these gambles paid off. I wasn't reckless. I was just... courageous, I guess you could say."

"Were you diagnosed with bipolar one, or bipolar two?" With bipolar one, the person would sometimes hallucinate, as if they were schizophrenic, which was why the two disorders were often confused with one another.

"Bipolar one."

"And did you hallucinate when you were manic?"

He shook his head. "I don't think so but the mania was usually colorful. I had such clarity. I miss that. I miss the clarity, the energy, and the feeling I could do anything. The feeling I was somebody who could conquer the entire world. But I don't miss the other parts of mania. The agitation, the anger."

Again with the anger. I had to find out what he was talking about. "So, when you were angry, how did you express it?"

"I would destroy things. Break things. Punch holes in the walls. Start fights. Scream at the top of my lungs at people."

He shook his head. "I wasn't too kind to the people I saw out in the world. If a waitress made one little mistake, I was screaming at her and making her cry. If a dry cleaner didn't have my suit ready at the time when they said that they would, I would go over there and rip them a new one in front of everybody. And yes, I probably wasn't so nice to Ava at that time."

"When you say the words 'not so nice to Ava at that time,' what do you mean?" I had to wonder if something was there.

Silas stared at me again with the same kind of stare that unnerved me when I first met him. It looked as if he was trying to decide whether to tell me the truth. "There were restraining orders."

I rolled back my chair. I was feeling a sense of anger. It seemed he was lying to me when he insisted he would never lay a hand on his wife. "Why were there restraining orders?"

"You have to understand something. I've been taking medicine for bipolar disorder for the past five years. So anything I'm telling you is old news. I'm a changed man. That's the reason why I didn't tell you about this. However, I know you'll find out about it sooner or later, so I might as well come out with it."

"I understand about bipolar disorder." I had never suffered from the disorder, thank God, but I knew people who did, including Harper. "I know that it means you're jumping out of your skin 24/7. I know it causes a heightened state of agitation and makes one very easily set off. Somebody looks at you wrong and it's off to the races. I know about that feeling. I've been there. So go ahead and tell me. I won't judge." I *did* know the feeling of being on a razor's edge, looking over into the abyss. I also knew the feeling of having an enormous amount of pent-up rage that bubbles up and finally explodes. I was there when I was a kid. I didn't have a chemical imbalance such as what causes bi-polar disorder, but I was dealing with an abusive stepfather and I feared for my life. So, I really did know how Silas was feeling when he had that period of unrestrained rage.

He finally just sighed. "I knew you would understand. I looked into your background, and I found out you've suffered hardships. I know about your stepfather and the fact that you killed him when you were 15. That's one of the reasons I hired you. I knew you would know what I was going through. But yes, there were incidents where my wife and I got physical."

"How physical?" I asked him.

"I beat her twice. The cops came to our house both times, but no arrests were made. The second time was when I got help. I loved her and was willing to do anything to make sure she stayed married to me. She told me she wanted me to see a psychiatrist, because she suspected there was something mentally wrong with me. She was concerned all along about the days when I would lock myself in my home office and not come out, because I was in there working day and night. I was working on problems concerning my company and I didn't want to be disturbed. During this time, I wouldn't eat or sleep for days on end. And when I would come out of the room, I would be at a heightened state of agitation, and that's when things would blow up. That happened several times, and the first time I beat her, she left the house and got a restraining order against me. She was gone for several weeks. In an apartment."

"Was she was in an apartment, or was she staying with her parents at the time?" I suddenly had a feeling the parents had more reason to hate him than what he had originally let on.

"She was staying at an apartment. She maintained a separate apartment for several years."

"And why did she maintain the separate apartment?"

"Because of the incidents when I would get angry and punch my hand through a wall. The reason why I punched my hand through a wall was to keep from hitting her, but I scared her all the same."

"And so when you say you scared her, what does that mean to you?"

"Well, sometimes I scared her but sometimes I just needed to leave. I just couldn't be around her. Everything she did was annoying to me, and anything she did wrong was a basis for me to scream at her. When I got like this, she would go to her apartment for a few days. She would come back in a couple of days and everything would be okay." He shook his head. "But they were never really okay. Not really. I mean, my periods of extreme mania when I was agitated would only last for a matter of days, and after that, things were not normal, but better. I mean, when I say that, it means I no longer had the urge to hit her, which is what I was always trying to stop myself from doing before. But I was having other issues. Granted, there were times when I was normal. When I was not depressed and not manic. I was just baseline. Those were the best times for us but I always felt my creativity was dulled during those times."

I made notes as he spoke. "So, there were times when things were normal and times when she had to be in a different apartment, because she couldn't be around you and you couldn't be around her. And twice you hit her. And did you have sex with other women during this time?"

"Yes. But that was never a problem. We had an open

relationship right from the start. You have to understand one thing - my wife has always had singular needs. Always. The two times when I actually beat on her, it was not okay with her, although if I would've done that to her while we were intimate, it would've been. It would've been consensual. But it wasn't. It wasn't consensual during those two times."

"I understand. So you had sex with other women during those times, and she had sex with other men too, right?"

"Yes. Just like it had always been in our relationship. That's what it was like before she died. In fact, when I was away in Europe for those six months, I knew she was seeing other men. In fact, she would call me and describe what those other men did to her and this would arouse me, which is why she did that."

"And did she describe the sex with these other men or would she describe them beating her?"

"Both."

"And did you get aroused by hearing about her having sex with these men, or by hearing about her describing the beatings these other men gave her?"

"Both." He studied me for a few minutes. "I know how it sounds, hearing that my wife was humiliated, degraded and beaten aroused me. I would apologize for this, but I don't see why I should. To each our own, live and let live and all that, right?"

"Right." I didn't really know what to say. I didn't really understand the mentality of people who get involved in an alternative lifestyle, but it wasn't for me to judge.

"So you're telling me, you saw a psychiatrist, and you started taking Geodon and Prozac, and that's got you on a more even keel?" I asked.

"That's exactly what I'm telling you."

I nodded. "I'm going to find out if you're lying," I said. "I hope you know that."

"I do."

I studied him. I still had a feeling he was hiding quite a lot, but I was getting somewhere with him and that slightly encouraged me.

## Chapter Five

THAT NIGHT I went home to talk to my kids. I had found out more about the kid with the gun, through Tom's investigation, and I found out the kid was disturbed, to say the very least. I knew disturbed. I was disturbed when I was a kid. I knew the feeling of desperately wanting to be heard by somebody, anybody, and knowing that nobody was paying attention to my cries for help. In a way, I could relate to that kid who brought the gun in. I *was* that kid when I was his age.

At the same time, I worried. The school were supposed to install metal detectors and there were also plans to make all the kids start bringing their books and supplies in clear backpacks, but I didn't think that was enough. I didn't want the teachers to be armed, nor did I particularly want a security guard to patrol the school - there was just too much possibility for a situation to get out of hand if there were armed personnel on school grounds. I wasn't quite sure what steps would be the best ones to take to keep my kids, and all the other kids, safe, but I knew there had to be a better solution for what was happening.

I needed to talk to Nate and Amelia about the situation further, to really get a gauge on where their heads were at on the situation. Nate was his usual laconic self, not wanting to talk about the student with the gun or anything else on his mind. Amelia didn't know much about the incident, because it didn't happen in her school, but I knew she was scared, too.

As their father, I was determined to get more out of my kids, especially Nate. God forbid that kid inherit my propensity for violence and mayhem. If he did, he might be the next shooter, for all I knew. I had to make sure that didn't happen, so I needed to get him to talk.

But, when I went home, I found something else that caught my attention. Something I wasn't necessarily expecting.

"This came for you," Nate said to me, handing me an envelope. The envelope belied nothing and didn't have a return address on it.

I took the envelope and hesitated. Nate was still just standing there, looking like he wanted to say something. I didn't press him, though. If there was one thing I learned from my family counselor, it was that Nate would talk to me in his time. I couldn't force things out of him, as much as I wanted to. As much as I desired to sit him down and not let him stand back up until he talked, I knew that pushing him would just make him get farther away from me. At some point, pushing Nate just might result in something I didn't want to deal with. Something that maybe I *couldn't* deal with. I didn't think he was capable of shooting me while I slept, as I did with my stepfather, but one never knows.

"Thanks," I said, looking at him. I waved the envelope

around for a few seconds while Nate just stood there, staring at the floor. I realized I was holding my breath as I waited for him to speak. "Uh, kid…"

"Well, I'll be upstairs in my room. Call me when it's dinnertime."

At that, he turned and walked into his room and shut the door.

I shook my head and sighed. He was close to talking to me, but something was holding him back. I wished I knew what it was, but maybe I would find out later.

In the meantime, I had to read this letter. I was genuinely curious on who wrote it.

## Chapter Six

*Dear Mr. Harrington,*
*You don't know me. In fact, I'm not going to tell you who I am. You may never find out. I know, I know, you will do your best to try to find out where this letter originated, but the origin of this letter won't tell you a thing. This letter was sent from a Kansas City Post Office, so what will that tell you? So, don't even try to find out my identity. I'm writing you this letter to tell you your client is guilty. I know him, and I knew Ava. I knew what kind of relationship they had. I know he tried to tell you he only beat her up twice, and the reason she had bruises on her arms recently was because she was going out having sex with other men and they were beating on her. I can definitively tell you that's not true.*
*Ava and Silas were not involved in the lifestyle. That dungeon he showed you wasn't a dungeon at all. It was simply a guest house, where servants were housed before Ava and Silas bought that house, and where guests stayed when they visited. That was it. No dungeon, no kinky sex implements were in there. I know you couldn't tell what that building was, because it burned to the ground, so the only thing left was the brick wall with the handcuffs attached and Ava's hands. I under-*

*stand what you probably believe, because that was what Silas told you. However, that's not what that house was used for. In fact, those handcuffs were just installed recently.*

*Silas would want you to believe that Ava was chained to that wall was because they were involved in consensual sexual play, but I can tell you that's not true. Talk to her parents. You'll get the story. You'll find out what their relationship was really like. He's trying to make himself look good by keeping those prescriptions for bi-polar disorder in his bathroom. However, he is not taking meds for his bipolar disorder. I do believe he has a mental illness, but he is not seeking treatment for it. He never has.*

*You'll see Ava had two restraining orders against him five years ago. She was terrified of your client, terrified he would kill her if she left him. Ironically, her rational fear for her life was what caused her to stay with him all these years. He threatened her life, told her he would find her, no matter where she was, and kill her if she left him and if she filed another restraining order against him. He's a very wealthy and powerful man, so Ava had reason to believe he would be as good as his word. That's the real reason why there's not been any restraining orders within the past five years, and that's the real reason why Ava stayed married to that monster.*

*Talk to her friends. Talk to her parents. You'll get the full story.*
*I can also tell you that Ava was not sick. I know that's another thing he was trying to tell you – she was sick. That she died before the fire had ever swept in. He told you he had no idea how she died, but she just went into cardiac arrest while he was having sex with her, and he couldn't revive her. To this, I ask you - don't you think that fire was a bit convenient? The fire burned her to the point where nobody could look for any kind of poison or any other way she might've died. That was by design. That was why he set that fire. He wanted everybody to believe the fire just happened. But it didn't just happen. There were accelerants, as you know. I believe Ava was burned to death, but, even if she wasn't, she died at his hand. Maybe he poisoned her, then*

*burned her body to ensure that no medical examiner could possibly discover the poison in Ava's system. I don't know, but what I do know is that Ava died at Silas' hand.*
*Do not be naïve. You are dealing with a very dangerous man. A very dangerous man.*

THE LETTER ENDED THERE. No signature, of course. I put my thumb and forefinger to the top of the nose and stared at the table where the letter was sitting.

Amelia came over to me. "What's wrong, Dad?" she asked me, putting her little arm around my back.

"Nothing. I just had to wonder if –" I took a deep breath. "I think I need to get off my new client's case."

I didn't know what to think. On the one hand, this person seemed to know an awful lot about the nature of Silas and Ava's relationship and the circumstance of Ava's death. The writer also seemed to believe the dungeon wasn't actually a dungeon. So what if it wasn't a dungeon? Seriously?

The significance of whether or not the building was a dungeon was that if it weren't, that would possibly call into question Silas' explanation for why Ava was chained to a wall. If that structure was a dungeon, then Silas chaining Ava to a wall would be easily explained. I never got into BDSM myself, but I was familiar with the lifestyle, and I knew that handcuffing partners to walls was something that was common play. It certainly wasn't unheard of.

But if it wasn't a dungeon, and Silas and Ava weren't in the lifestyle…that would be cause for concern, to say the very least. If they weren't in the lifestyle, then I would have to question Silas' story, all of it. I would have to question why Ava really was chained to that wall. I would also have to question why Ava recently had bruises on her arms. If she wasn't in the lifestyle, then she wouldn't be seeking sex partners to beat on her, would she? And she also wouldn't be consenting to Silas beating her if she wasn't into submission. If the two weren't involved in BDSM, I would have to conclude that everything Silas told me was a lie and I would be back to square one.

I shook my head. That letter certainly did complicate matters, to say the least.

## Chapter Seven

LATER THAT NIGHT, I hired my baby-sitter to watch Nate and Amelia, and went to meet Nick out at a bar. I would have to hire him to help me try to figure out what was going on in this case.

I got to our bar and he was sitting in the back, waving a beer at me. "Buddy," he said, as I sat down. Nick was doing well, very well, on the outside. He was keeping his nose clean and was really loving the investigation work he was doing with Tom Garrett at his side. Like Tom, he knew many of the key players on the street, for he was one of them and the street guys knew it. That generally meant he had an easier time getting them to talk than somebody would who had never on the inside. "What's going on?"

I sat down and ordered a beer. "Nothing," I said. "But I wanted to show you this letter and ask you what you thought about it."

I handed him the letter and he read it. Then he shook his head. "I wouldn't be overly concerned about this," he said. "I mean, it could have been written by anybody. The media has been like flies on shit with this case, breathlessly reporting every detail. The person who wrote this might have been a crank with an imagination. It's not like they're spouting top-secret information here. Or, who knows, it might even be the person responsible for all this, assuming your client isn't."

"I know. I know what you're saying. Obviously, somebody is trying to throw me off the track. But the problem with this letter is that it's just validating some of the doubts I have about this case. I mean, the letter-writer makes a point – it *was* convenient that the fire was such a wildfire, to the point where it burned down everything in that dungeon. I mean, I couldn't really tell if it was actually a dungeon. Silas told me they had implements in this dungeon that were typical for people into the BDSM lifestyle – the St. Andrew's Cross, whipping posts and things like that. All conveniently made of wood. But everything in that structure was completely burned, so the only thing that was still intact was a single brick wall with the handcuffs and those hands. The whole thing just seems way too convenient. He knew I would want reasons for why she got restraining orders against him, and why her parents saw bruises on her body, so he could just be cooking up this whole story to try to explain these things away. At least, that's what this letter implies. I don't know what to believe."

Nick shook his head and took a swig of his drink. "All I'm saying is that perhaps you need to just keep an open mind about your client's claims. Don't jump to conclusions. You're a criminal defense attorney. You know there are probably people who have it in for your client and will try to throw you off. Just go along with your investigation and try not to give this letter too much credence. I mean, if this person was somebody with actual information for you, they should step forward. Not send some kind of anonymous letter. Don't you think?"

Nick was right about that. If anything, it made me suspect there was more to the story, that maybe somebody else actually was behind it all. This letter was the kind of letter I would expect to receive from somebody trying to frame my client. I would have to take everything with a grain of salt.

I looked at the letter, thinking it was something impossible to trace – if it was an email, or a text message, then it would be traceable. Even if the person went to lengths to hide their identity, I could still get Anna to find out who sent it. That wasn't the case with this letter, though. I tried to trace the origin, but all I could tell was that it was sent through a public mailbox in South Kansas City. That, unfortunately, told me nothing. It didn't even give me a clue on where the person might live, because, if he or she was smart, he or she wouldn't send the letter from a mailbox in their neighborhood.

I tucked the letter into my briefcase and decided to just forget about it. Not that I would ignore it and not follow up on the claims it made – of course I would, I had to – but it was just one more piece of evidence. I would have to find out from Ava's parents what kind of relationship Silas and Ava had. I would go through Ava's medical records to find out if she was really sick. The letter also stated that Silas wasn't really seeking treatment for bi-polar disorder, which would imply he had other mental problems, possibly, which weren't amenable to medicines. He told me he was angry and violent when he was younger, but he essentially eliminated his rage with bi-polar medicine. Was that a lie? Bi-polar disorder would be the perfect cover for a more sinister reason for why he spent time in a mental hospital.

Perhaps the bi-polar story was just that - a story. Maybe he was trying to manipulate me into thinking he was getting treatment for his mental illness and he was essentially all better. I had no doubt that Silas had some kind of mental illness, but whether or not it was an illness that could be controlled, as with bi-polar, or something that wasn't so easily controlled, like a personality disorder, remained to be seen.

"Well, I'm going to take this letter with a grain of salt. I won't ignore it. I will try to follow up, if only to find out the letter isn't true. At the same time, I'll come up with my own decisions and judgment about my client, after I speak with Ava's parents and friends, not to mention when I get Silas' records about his mental illness." I took a sip of my beer. "For now, I have to deal with a traumatized kid who won't speak to me. I'm sure you heard about the kid who brought a gun into Nate's school?"

Nick just shook his head. "I did, and thank God that kid seemed to not be serious about that gun. If he was, who knows what would have happened? All I can tell you is that it's a fucked-up world if there are elementary school kids bringing guns onto campus. Even more of a fucked-up world then the one you and I grew up in."

"I know. I never had to deal with this when I was growing up. I don't know what gets into these kids. I wish I did. All I know is that nobody seems to be safe. Not even kids in exclusive public schools. I certainly didn't think that sending my kids to private schools meant they would be safe. Nobody is really safe. I know that, but sometimes I try to pretend they are. Then, something like this happens, and, just like that, my bubble is popped. I'm not going to say I'm freaked out, because I still know the odds are astronomically against either of my kids being shot in school, but I am a bit concerned." I shook my head. "Then again, the kids have better odds of dying by being hit by a school bus or something like that, but I don't worry about that as much. Human psychology, I guess."

Nick nodded. "I know, it's weird. People die by the thousands, every day, in accidents, car accidents and otherwise. Very few kids end up getting shot in school. Yet, school violence is so sensationalized in the media, you start to think that every kid going to school will end up being a victim to something like this. I know you know that's not true. I know also you're afraid for your kids, but don't do anything rash. They're in the right schools." He took a sip of his beer. "And you can't keep them on a short leash. The last thing you want is to become one of those busy-body parents who try to control everything that happens to your kids. Let them live their lives. Odds are great they'll end up just fine. Especially Amelia - she kicked cancer, so that girl is tough. Nothing will take her out."

I laughed as I realized I was in danger of becoming a helicopter parent if I wasn't too careful. If I tried to control what happened to my kids, I would end up suffocating them, and that was the last thing I wanted to do.

"I know what you're saying," I said. "The last thing I want is to become one of those parents who lean on teachers all the time, demanding that they changed my child's grade for something. Somebody who tries to keep their kids on short leashes, so their possibilities will be limited when they grow up. I want them both to be sufficient, independent kids and adults. I want them to run the world someday. They could never do that if I'm going to try to control them, so I just have to let them be." Another sip of beer. "Turns out The Beatles knew what they were talking about when they said 'let it be.' Philosophers, they were."

"True that," Nick said. "Let it be. Whatever happens, happens. Man, I know how much you want to control them, if only because you want to prevent them from making the same mistakes you made. Trust me, I know. But this matter is just something you're going to have to live with. We are in a different world these days, a different time. As wild as we were, we were nothing compared to the kids of today. Cold comfort, I know, but you just have to play the odds and realize your kids most likely won't end up being killed in their schools. Some kids do, I know. It happens. But it probably won't happen here, and you can't let the possibility that it might happen get you down, buddy. Really, life is too damned short for such worries."

I smiled. "Oh, you speak the truth. Okay, well, let's try to brainstorm on this Silas thing. Do your research, and I'll do mine, and I'll try to figure out just what happened here."

"Will do, buddy, will do."

## Chapter Eight

I DECIDED that before I paid a visit to Ava's parents, I first would pay a visit to Silas' parents. I wanted to get a fuller picture of my client, before I went to Ava's family to try to get a fuller picture of her.

I drove to the house of Mr. and Mrs. Porter, which was in an older neighborhood in South Kansas City. This was a neighborhood that profoundly changed over the years. Back in the day, a thriving shopping mall was within blocks of this street, along with a host of restaurants – Olive Garden, Red Lobster, Applebee's, TGI Friday's, and other casual chains. The mall was at capacity with its stores, with large anchor stores that included Macy's, Jones and JC Penney's, and it was largely considered to be "the place to go" for people living in the South Kansas City area. The movie theater would pack them in to see new movies, such as *The Empire Strikes Back* and *Close Encounters of the Third Kind*. There was also a free-standing movie theater just down the road a bit that also packed kids in on the weekends, with lines forming on the street. Also in the neighborhood was what was known as a "hyper-mart" – this was back when Walmart was just starting to became the behemoth it was, and it anchored a shopping district that included many thriving stores, from a Best Buy to a Toys 'R' Us, to sporting goods big-box chains.

However, around the mid 80s to the early 1990s, everything changed. Shootings happened in the mall parking lot, and gangs moved in and took over. The anchor stores fled, leaving large empty buildings at each ends of the once-powerful and thriving mall. Eventually, the mall was razed, leaving nothing but an empty field. There was talk of redeveloping the area with a soccer stadium, but that fell through. When the mall closed, so did the restaurants, one by one. The Red Lobster building was still standing, as was the Olive Garden building, but they were now empty and lifeless, just like the neighborhood itself. Then the Hyper-mart went out of business, along with all the other stores around it. The Best Buy, the sporting goods store, the toy store, the eyeglass place, the gym, the restaurants - they were all gone.

The closing of the mall was the beginning of the end for this sad neighborhood. What was once a haven for working-class families was now a distressed area with run-down properties and little hope. Weeds grew up high on people's lawns, several houses had boarded-up windows, and there was even a drug house or two on the block. The Porter's house was no different. It was a ranch-style home, probably about 1000 square feet, with shutters that desperately needed painting and overgrown weeds on their front lawn.

I knocked on the door. I knew they were expecting me, as I called them this morning.

A lady answered my knock. It was impossible to know how old she was – she could have been in her 50s, 60s or 70s. Her hair was short, but she looked like she had slept in curlers. She had deep lines around her mouth and eyes and her skin looked like orange leather. She was still in her bathrobe, which was long with a floral pattern.

The thing that struck me most about this woman was she looked sad - as if she had long since given up. When she answered the door, she barely nodded, as that seemed to take too much effort. She stepped aside, allowing me into her living room, which was tiny. The furniture consisted of an ancient gold couch, a non-matching love-seat in worn pleather and an old recliner. None of it matched and, even though the furniture was sparse, it still overwhelmed this tiny room. She had a couple of dogs who were sitting on the couch, and they both wagged their tails when I came in the door.

She looked apologetic. "I know this place doesn't look like much, but it's all we can afford. Can I get you a cup of tea?"

I nodded, trying to be polite. "I would appreciate that very much." I looked around, seeing that the ceiling had water stains on it, which meant the roof was leaking, and I imagined there soon would be mold on the walls from the water. It didn't appear this woman did much to try to prevent the water from coming in - there wasn't even a bucket on the floor to catch it, so the carpet was soaked in spots and smelled like mildew.

She bustled around the kitchen and then brought out a floral pitcher that had steam coming out of its neck. She poured a cup for us both. "I understand you are representing my son on a murder charge," she said, then shook her head. "I never quite understood him. When I heard about the charge, I was not entirely surprised. I somehow always knew it might come to this with him."

I was curious about what she just said. What kind of mother would admit to "always knowing" her son would one day be arrested for murder? "I'm so sorry, but what did you mean by that? You always knew Silas would one day be arrested for murder?"

"Well, he's had a very troubled life. We took him in as a foster child when he was only seven years old. I wanted nothing more than to give him a chance. Before I met him, he had such little chance in life."

This was definitely a new piece of information for me. Silas had never told me he was in foster care, and he certainly never told me he was adopted by his parents.

"I'm so sorry, I guess I wasn't aware Silas was in foster care and was adopted. Can you tell me what the circumstances were? How you came upon him?"

She shook her head. "Bob and me, we tried for many years to have a child of our own. But it just didn't work. I guess it just wasn't meant to be. God just didn't want me to have children of my own. I guess I was always meant to be a foster mom and an adoptive mom. Like they always say, God never gives us more than we can handle, so I knew that when I got Silas in my house, even though he had some very special challenges, I was meant to handle them for him. I was meant to be his mother. I truly believe that."

I wondered what kind of "special challenges" she was talking about. "So tell me the circumstances. Why was he in foster care, and how did you end up with him in your home?"

She sighed. "Well, here's what the deal was. Silas' biological father was a very troubled man. He set fire to the family home while Silas's mother was asleep. She was killed in that fire. Silas himself managed to get out of the house, without any burns, which was a miracle. All this happened to him long before I ever knew him - when he was only five years old. I guess his birth father was a schizophrenic hearing voices that told him he had to burn down the house. The reason why Silas was able to get out was that his bedroom door opened into the backyard. His mother wasn't so lucky. Silas' father was institutionalized and then Silas himself went from one foster home to another for a few years before I got to him. His therapists told me he was suffering from Attachment Disorder. Do you know what that is?"

"I believe so." From what I understood, attachment disorder occurred when a child does not bond with anybody when he or she is very young. However, I wasn't quite clear on what the particulars were of someone who suffered from this disorder. I understood that, amongst other symptoms, the person who suffered from Attachment Disorder didn't always develop much of a conscience and they often had problems with trusting people. They usually had problems, in general, with forming lasting relationships with other people.

She shook her head again. "I did my best with him. I know I tried. But the damage was done by what happened long before I ever knew him. Growing up, he was just very hard to control. Thank God he was smart and was able to get it together enough to be very successful."

"What kind of problems did you have with him when he was young?"

She took a sip of her tea. "There were problems around the neighborhood and the cops came to our door several times. There were a lot of burglaries, people breaking into cars, that sort of thing. Nobody could say for sure that Silas was involved in any of it, but I could never control him. From the time he was 10 years old, he was running away from home and we were always looking for him. He would disappear for a day or two, and would come back, as if nothing ever happened. In the meantime, crimes would happen around the neighborhood, and they usually occurred when Silas was not in the house."

I made notes as she spoke. "Was he ever arrested for any of these crimes? Did he ever go into juvy or anything like that?"

"No, but I think it's just because he was too smart to get caught doing what he was doing. That was the one thing about Silas - he has a genius level IQ. Just off the charts. He was so smart that I enrolled him in college when he was only 15 years old. It was a relief, to get him out of the house, to be perfectly honest with you. His test scores were so high that he went to the local university, UMKC. As you probably know, he ended up getting a PhD at Stanford. That's because of his scores on his Graduate Record Exam. He scored perfect on all the sections. Plus, he managed a 4.0 GPA at the university even though he never studied. I know that him going to college at such a young age saved him. It gave him a purpose in life. At least that's what the psychologist said – she told me that part of the reason why he was running away, and getting in so much trouble, was because he was so bored. School bored him and he was just going out of his mind."

I wondered if this was significant that Silas went to college at such a young age and the fact he had such a high IQ. I knew he was intelligent – you don't become a billionaire before the age of 35 if you're a dummy. Especially a self-made one. So that part of what she was telling me was not surprising at all. What was surprising was the trouble he got into. "Let me ask you something. Were there any suspicious fires set around the neighborhood that the police questioned Silas about?"

She appeared to think about it for a second. Then she shook her head. "No, I don't believe there were. At least not in this neighborhood. I can't tell you if other neighborhoods might have had some suspicious fires that maybe Silas was involved in as a young child. When he would run away, he could have possibly gone to other neighborhoods and set fires. I don't know."

"And you say Silas was diagnosed when he was young with attachment disorder. You also talked about a therapist. Did you take him to this therapist?"

She nodded. "I had a court-appointed therapist assigned to Silas when he first came to live with us. That was because Silas had special mental health needs. I was able to take him to a therapist once a week. She diagnosed him with the attachment disorder. She told me I would possibly have problems with him as far as him not having empathy for others, not being able to trust, and not being able to bond with me or Bob. And, sure enough, that's what happened. Silas was never somebody cuddly. He was always very standoffish. He was never one to show affection. He was always very... remote. He wasn't a bad kid. He just didn't have very authentic emotions. I think that's probably the best way to describe him. I mean, he could put on a face when people came over. But it wasn't real. You have to understand, because he was so intelligent, he could think his way through social situations, if that means anything at all."

I think I knew what she was talking about. That was the way some people were, if they suffered from narcissistic personality disorder, antisocial personality disorder or something of the sort. I knew this, because I had done research on all these disorders and psychology was my minor in college. My knowledge of psychology had always helped me in my job of being a criminal defense attorney. Lack of empathy was the hallmark of many personality disorders, and I wondered if Silas was not suffering from bipolar disorder at all, but something else. Some kind of personality disorder. If that were true, the situation just got more complicated. In the meantime, I would have to brush up on what the symptoms were of someone suffering from attachment disorder.

"What else can you tell me about Silas? Do you know anything about his relationship with Ava?"

She looked sad again. "I'm afraid I can't tell you much about that. You see, Silas decided when he got out of Stanford that he didn't want to have a thing to do with me or Bob anymore. I think we embarrass him. You have to understand that Silas feels he has a certain image to uphold to the world. And having parents like us, living hand to mouth, in a tiny little house like this, it did not fit in with the image he wanted to portray to the world. So he stopped answering my phone calls." At that, she got out a box of Kleenex and blew her nose. I could see tears in her eyes. "I suppose I don't blame him. I mean, Bob and me, we never had much. Bob works a lot. He has several jobs. In fact, he's at work right now, at the local Walmart, as a part-time job. He got laid off his job at the factory several years ago. Since then, he's been working part-time jobs and so have I. I work the night shift at a local Denny's as a waitress and I clean office buildings in the mornings. Bob works at Walmart and as a cook at the same Denny's I work at. Thank God this house is paid for, otherwise I think the two of us would probably be homeless."

I suddenly got a different picture of my client. Here he

was, a billionaire, while his father was working part-time at Walmart and at Denny's, his mother was working part-time at Denny's and cleaning office buildings, and his mother was saying that if they didn't have the house paid for, they would be homeless. What kind of son would just ignore his parents like that? Especially when it seemed as if his parents had nothing but love for him. These parents saved him from being in the foster care system, yet he now just ignored them?

I supposed that went along with Silas apparently having a lack of empathy or a conscience. Because only somebody who didn't have empathy or conscience would do that to their parents. When a person has money to spare, yet they don't spare any of it on the people who raised them...I had no use for people like that. My own mother didn't live much better - she lived in a trailer and she, too, worked at Walmart. But I tried to give her money. She just refused to take it. I also tried to make sure her car was in good shape, as I changed her oil and rotated and inflated her tires whenever I saw her, and I also always took a look under her hood. Plus, I did basic repairs around her place. That was all she allowed me to do, however. I wanted to do more.

Apparently, Silas didn't want to even do that for his parents. Judging from the way the place looked, I knew Silas probably didn't do any repairs around this house.

Arlene appeared to read my mind. "I know what you're thinking. You're thinking our son has billions of dollars, so he really should help us out financially. I suppose you're probably right. At the same time, we don't expect it. We don't ask for it either. But it would be nice to get some new furniture for this place and some new carpeting." She looked down at the patches in her carpet that were worn so thin you could see the floor underneath. "As you can probably tell, this carpet has not been changed for many years and it was cheap to begin with. I think the last time the carpet was new in this house was in the 1970s. There's a lot we would like to have, but, at the same time, Silas doesn't owe us anything."

"No offense, but how can you say that? You saved him from foster care and did your best with raising him. And this is how he treats you?"

She looked at a Kleenex, and held it in her hands, wringing it over and over again. "He's a good boy. I know he's had a lot of problems, but he's a good boy." That was all she said. She didn't address my question directly. Probably because she didn't have a good answer for why Silas would be so negligent and downright cruel to his parents.

I decided I wouldn't get anywhere with that line of questioning, so I changed the subject. "So, I guess you don't know anything about Silas' relationship with Ava, then?" I knew that since Silas had apparently cut off communication with his parents when he went to Stanford, it was probably true that Arlene did not know about Silas' life with Ava. I had already read in his bio he had attended Stanford, after graduating from UMKC at the age of 18. He graduated from Stanford with a PhD at age 22 and met Ava when he was 25. I had a feeling Arlene probably couldn't tell me anything about Silas' relationship with Ava for that reason alone. However, maybe she didn't have to. She told me enough when she explained how Silas treated her and her husband.

I was starting to think that Silas might be somebody as dangerous as what that letter said. There was one thing I knew about people who had personality disorders - oftentimes it was coupled with a sense of rage, which could be a very dangerous combination indeed. I would have to find out exactly what the deal was with Silas' mental issues.

What I did know was that, to say the very least, Silas was a very crappy son.

Whether or not that meant anything for this case, I didn't know.

## Chapter Nine

AFTER SPEAKING TO ARLENE, I went to my office to do some research on Attachment Disorder before heading home. I felt so sorry for his mother. She seemed like such a nice lady and such a hard worker. She didn't have a lot of breaks in her life, but she obviously was full of love. She adopted Silas when he was only seven years old, knowing he had special needs, and knowing that because of his background, with his father killing his mother in such a way, he would be a handful, to say the very least. And he was. It sounded like he gave his mother a lot of grief, and yet, the second he became somebody, he just ignored her and her husband.

His mom and dad.

That made me sick.

I also called Anna. I would have to see if she could get the records for Silas' early life before doing the research on this disorder. I knew I could get the records if I did a full request for them, as I had a full waiver from Silas for medical records, but I didn't have time for that. I wanted to get my hands on these records so I could know a little bit more about who, exactly, I was dealing with. I had a feeling that probably Arlene herself didn't have the full story on what had happened when Silas was a young boy.

I got Anna working on finding those records, and I sat back in my chair. It would just be a few minutes before she would be emailing them to me.

I was right about that, as the email came in not 10 minutes later.

I got to the email attachment and read the information about Silas and his birth father and mother.

It turned out Anna did me one better. She found the psychiatric records for Silas' birth father. Arlene told me that Silas' birth father was suffering from schizophrenia. That's what these records seem to indicate, and the records also seemed to indicate that Silas' birth father was still institutionalized after all these years.

For about an hour, I read about all the incidents that his birth father, Jude Devereux, was involved with over the years. It seemed he burned down the house because a voice was telling him to do that. For many years, he was a violent man, and for most of those years, he had been homeless. According to these records, Silas' father had been involved in arson-related incidents when he was in his 20s and he went into a mental institution after that, but he was out after just a few years. He got out of the mental institution at 31 and then met Silas' mother, whose name was Annette. According to the records, Jude was apparently in remission for five years, during which he didn't have any kind of schizophrenic episodes. However, the remission ended when the voices came back, and his father ended up setting fire to the house and killing his wife, Silas' mother.

At the moment, Jude was in an institution for the criminally insane. He was currently being housed in the Missouri state hospital, in Fulton Missouri, which was in the rural part of the state, a good three hours away from where I lived. However, I would try to visit him as well.

As I read the information on Silas' early life, I realized that long before his father set fire to the house, he was having problems. Jude Devereux might've been technically in remission from his schizophrenia but it was plain he was still not mentally sound. For years, he had been extremely abusive to both his wife and his young son. Family services had been called to the house many times, and there were several times when the social worker who visited had recommended that Silas be taken from the home.

Even though I resented Silas for being so cruel to his adoptive parents, I also felt sorry for him. His early upbringing was much like mine, and I knew how painful that was to grow up that way. According to his therapist's records, when he was a young boy, he didn't have a chance to really bond with anybody. His mother was too terrified of his father to really have the mental energy to care for Silas, and his father was obviously suffering from extreme mental illness.

I then looked at the records that indicated his therapist had diagnosed Silas with Attachment Disorder when he was five years old. That was the first time he had been taken into foster care, because that was when his mother had been killed by his father. Apparently, in the two years between that first foster home, and his going to stay with Arlene and Bob, he had seen a court-appointed therapist many times.

And then I saw the line that made my blood run cold. *Silas has shown an unhealthy fascination with fire.* Those were the words that his therapist had written down.

*Silas has shown an unhealthy fascination with fire.*

And as I read through some of the symptoms of people who suffer from Attachment Disorder, I learned about some of the symptoms. Along with having problems with trust, problems with empathy, and problems with relating to people, people who suffer from this disorder also often show other symptoms.

One of them was fascination with fire.

Was it a coincidence that Ava was killed in a fire?

Or was it something else?

## Chapter Ten

THE NEXT DAY, I knew I had to do one thing, and that was to pay a visit to Silas' father before talking to Ava's parents to see what they had to say about Ava's relationship with Silas. I'd gotten a better picture of my client by speaking with his adoptive mother. I felt I had to see his birth father to see for myself what kind of person he was and I hoped he could also give me some insight on the kind of person Silas was. Who he was.

The Fulton State Hospital is the state hospital in Fulton Missouri, which is almost smack-dab in the middle of the state. I took a look at this hospital, realizing it looked just like a prison, which is what it was, for the most part. After all, it housed the criminally insane - the criminals too insane to try or were adjudged to be insane by a jury of their peers. I knew how difficult it was to successfully argue an insanity plea - you had to not know what you were doing at the time you committed the crime, or not know what you were doing was a crime.

The Fulton State Hospital was a place for people who

murdered others, not realizing murder was against the law or not knowing that what they were doing actually was murder. People like Andrea Yates, who killed her five children in a psychotic fugue while suffering under religious delusions. People like John Hinckley Jr., who attempted to assassinate Ronald Reagan because he wanted to impress the actress Jody Foster. Generally, the institution for the criminally insane housed people like this. I therefore knew Jude Devereux would be somebody who wasn't in touch with reality, to say the least. Still, I wanted to see him for myself.

The hospital was situated behind a large barbed-wire fence. It was built in 1800s and it looked like it. It was enormous, made with red brick, and its facade made the structure look foreboding and depressing at the same time. I had been to sanitariums like this before. When I was in high school, I took a field trip to a mental institution and was horrified by some of the rooms they showed me. It seemed as if that hospital had been around since the 1800s as well, and I thought that if there were ghosts who roamed the halls, they would tell you stories about shock therapy that would often break the patient's back and being strapped into chairs to keep them from hurting themselves. They could also tell you about any number of crude procedures performed on the criminally insane throughout the years, like lobotomies and procedures like submerging the insane into cold baths for long periods of time.

As I approached the entrance to this hospital, I realized it was much the same as the hospital I visited long ago on that field trip. If these walls could talk, they would probably howl and scream.

I went right up to the admissions officer, and told her I wanted to see Silas's father, Jude Devereux.

"Do you have an appointment?" The girl was young and blonde and looked like she wanted to be anywhere but where she was, not that I blamed her. This place was even more depressing than a regular hospital, and, for me, that said a lot.

"No, I don't." And I showed her my bar card. "I'm an attorney in the middle of a criminal investigation involving my client, Silas Porter. Jude Devereux is the father of my client and I really need to see him. If that's possible." I knew that because I was a professional and a lawyer, I wouldn't have a problem unless Jude was still deemed to be dangerous. However, from what I understood from Anna's records she sent me, Jude had been heavily medicated and had not had a dangerous episode for many years. So I imagined he was still somebody who I could see and hopefully speak with.

She nodded. "Since you're an attorney, and it seems as if Jude Devereux is not somebody who has been dangerous, it shouldn't be a problem for you to see him. However, I would like for you to be accompanied by a doctor. Let me just notify the doctor on call." She looked at her file and then she chose a doctor who could go with me to see Jude. "Dr. Riley is the doctor on call on that ward. Just a second while I call him." At that, she got on the phone, and she looked at me. "Dr. Riley will be right with you."

In about 10 minutes, Dr. Riley appeared before me. He was a tall, thin man, with a mop of curly hair and glasses perched on his long nose. He saw me and extended his hand. "I'm Dr. Evan Riley, and I will accompany you to see Mr. Devereux."

I stood up. "Thank you for accommodating me. It's very nice to meet you. I realize this is on short notice so I very much appreciate it."

He nodded. "Well this is a fairly common thing. We get criminal defense attorneys in here quite frequently, so this is not something out of the ordinary at all. I understand you are representing the biological son of Mr. Devereux. Is that true?"

"Yes, that's true."

"Well, of course I can't tell you any details about Mr. Devereux's condition. That's strictly confidential. But I can tell you that Mr. Devereux is not lucid but he's not dangerous. This has been his condition, off and on, for quite a few years now. He has been one of our better patients, to be honest with you."

I wondered why Jude Devereux was still in the mental hospital. Anna would have to get into it to find out that information. From what I understood, he was not convicted for murdering his wife because he was judged insane when this happened, so he was adjudged to be not guilty by reason of insanity. Because of that, he had come to this place instead of being sent to prison. But if he hadn't been dangerous for many years, he might be eligible for release. Then again, a woman was dead because of him and a house was burned to the ground. It probably wasn't simple to get him out of this place, no matter how mild-mannered he had been acting.

I followed Dr. Riley to a room and he opened up the door. I saw a man who I assumed to be Jude. He was a slight man, completely bald, with green eyes that bugged out of his head as if he had some kind of hyper-thyroid issue like Graves' Disease. He appeared to have dentures instead of teeth, as his choppers were perfect and white. He shared a room with a red-headed man who was catatonic and laying in his bed.

Jude saw me coming in and he stood up and smiled.

"Jude," Dr. Riley said. "This is —" he looked at me and shook his head. "I'm so sorry, this is so unprofessional of me, but I didn't get your name."

I smiled, realizing this was a mistake I made a million times myself. "Damien Harrington," I said as pleasantly as possible.

"This is Damien Harrington," Dr. Riley said to Jude. "He's an attorney."

Jude just smiled and held out his hand, and I shook it. "Very nice to meet you," he said to me. "Want to sit down?"

"Thank you very much." I sat down in a plastic chair next to a small table where Jude apparently had been working a large jigsaw puzzle. "Mr. Devereux, I'm representing your biological son, Silas Porter, in a criminal matter."

"Son? I don't remember having a son." He shook his head. "I don't know what you're talking about. I don't have a son."

I was confused at first, but then I suddenly realized what happened. I knew Dr. Riley couldn't explain what kind of treatments Jude had received over the years but I had the feeling that electro-shock therapy probably was administered quite a few times. If they did this often enough, Jude might not have memories of what had happened before he started receiving his treatments. Amnesia was a common side effect from these kinds of treatments.

This would be more complicated than I thought. "Mr. Devereux, do you remember why you are here?" I asked him.

He shook his head. "I don't know. I don't know why I'm here. All I know is I've been here for as long as I can remember. Why I'm here, I don't know."

"So you don't remember anything about the fire?"

He looked at me with blank eyes. "Fire? What do you mean fire? What are you talking about?"

I looked over at Dr. Riley to see if he was giving me any kind of warning, but he wasn't. "Mr. Devereux, you have a son, his name is Silas, and he has been accused of murder. You haven't seen him since he was a little boy. If you don't remember having a son –"

He looked at Dr. Riley. "Dr. Riley, can I please speak with this gentleman in private?" he asked the doctor politely.

I looked at Dr. Riley. "I hope you don't mind."

He nodded. "If you have any issues, here's the button you push." He showed me a little red button attached to the bed. "Somebody will be just around the corner."

I felt a little out of sorts that we had to have a panic button, but, then again, I supposed that was how it was in this facility.

Once the doctor left, Jude lowered his voice. "Are you sure there's not anybody around who can hear us?" He shook his head. "You never know when the government will be listening to you. You just never know when the FBI might be coming to your door, wanting to manipulate your thoughts for their own gain. You know that happens, don't you? You do know government agencies can share your thoughts and change your ideas, and they can arrest you without a warrant? Did you know there are gulags where they put people who think these criminal thoughts? I'll bet you didn't know any of that. I'll bet you didn't know our government is up to such terrible things. But I know. I know it all. That's why I'm here. I'm here because somebody high up, somebody powerful, wanted to shut me up. So they put me in here. That's why I want to make sure there's nobody around who can listen to me."

I nodded, not saying a word that would contradict his delusions. It was pointless to talk sensibly to somebody living in an alternate reality, so I didn't even try. I had a difficult enough time trying to talk sense into people who weren't actively schizophrenic. "No, I didn't know about the gulags, and I didn't know the government —"

"Shhhh…. Listen, if you say things too loud in here, you'll have thirty men on your tail like white on rice. You're already in danger because you're here with me." He pointed up at the ceiling. "You can't see them, but there's listening devices in that ceiling and somebody is always listening to everything I say. They report everything directly to Washington. I'm a dangerous person. And now you're in here talking to me, so they're gonna think you're also a dangerous person. Just fair warning."

I leaned back in my chair. "Mr. Devereux, do you really not remember you have a son?"

He leaned in close to me. And then he spoke in a whisper. "Of course I remember I have a son. I just didn't want to say that in front of a doctor. I have to speak in a whisper, because I'm afraid the people from the government, if they find out I have a son, they're going to come after him next. They're going to start harassing him and try to get him to give them information about me." He nodded with a smile. "Yes, I know I have a son. I haven't seen him since he was five years old, but I know I have one."

"So what do you know about him?"

"Are you asking me if I think he has the same kinds of problems I have?"

I felt confused. Did he realize he had problems? Was he experiencing a brief period of lucidity? Or was he just talking about something else? "What kind of problems do you have?" I asked him.

"Problems with having the government listening to my every word. I can't help that I'm such a powerful and dangerous person to the United States government that they have to keep me here. And I know about my Silas. I know about him. I've been following his story over the years. And I know he has become a very wealthy and powerful man himself. And that scares me. He's so rich that…" He lowered his voice again.

"He's so rich that I know the government will want to shut him down. Plus, he's been developing new technologies. These technologies scare the people in the government. They don't want his technologies known to the public. They want to shut him down because he's my son. That's all I can really tell you."

I shook my head. I should've known he wasn't referencing his schizophrenia when he indicated he had problems. He wasn't that self-aware.

He smiled. "Don't you think I know about what happened with Silas and his wife? Did you know I know he's been framed for murder? Know all about it. Know all about what happened with him and his wife. I've been reading about it in the paper. Somebody set that fire. It wasn't my son. I think that somebody else set that fire. Set that fire so he could go to prison for the rest of his life." He nodded and lowered his voice to a whisper again. "The government wants him out of the way so they want him to go to prison. They hired somebody to frame my son for killing his wife. I guarantee you that's just what happened. It was the same with me. I was framed so I could be locked up for the rest of my life. They want to shut up people like us. We know too much."

I was confused again. I didn't know how he knew so much about Silas and how he could process information about him. "When Silas was a little boy, do you remember anything about living with him and his mother?"

"Yes. Of course I do. What do you need to know?"

"Did you notice any kinds of problems, like maybe he was acting out in school, or something like that?"

He shook his head. "Silas was a very bright boy. He was only five years old when I last saw him and was already in the third grade. He just leapfrogged in front of everybody. And yes, he had a lot of problems in school. Of course he did. He was much younger than all the other kids in his class, and much smarter than them, so he was a lot smaller than all of his classmates. So he started fights. Lots of fights." He smiled. "I'm afraid he might be too much like his old man."

"What else can you tell me about him?"

He sighed. "I can't tell you anything. What I can tell you is I don't –" He paused, looked up at the ceiling, and then lowered his voice. "I don't belong here. I'm just here because I was protecting my son. I was protecting my son. And nobody can ever tell me I did the wrong thing."

I wondered what he was talking about. "What do you mean, you were just protecting your son?"

"Listen, I know I would have ended up here sooner or later, even if I didn't take the fall for my son. Sooner or later, I would've ended up here because they want me in here, so I don't regret what I did for him. Not at all. The people in the government, they want me in here. So I knew that when I told the police I set the fire, and not my son, I was doing the right thing."

I swallowed hard. I got the gist of what he was saying, but I didn't really want to acknowledge it. Yet it was staring me in the face. "Are you saying Silas set the fire that killed his own mother?"

He just stared at me. "I've said too much. I don't want my son to get in more trouble."

I blinked my eyes. On the one hand, this man was clearly delusional and was suffering from schizophrenia. He had a multitude of paranoid fantasies. So I didn't know if I could believe him.

Yet, what if it was true? This man was strangely lucid when he spoke about his son. He knew all about Silas being accused of murder. And it was certainly possible that a five-year-old boy, with an extremely high IQ, and an attachment disorder, could have done that to his mother. I had seen stranger things. Plus, his therapist indicated that Silas had an unhealthy interest in fire.

I thought about what his adoptive mother said to me about the night Silas' mother died. She told me that Silas could get out of the house because his bedroom door opened up into the backyard, so he could walk out of there. But his mother was not so lucky. Her bedroom did not face the backyard. In fact, she was on the third story.

Was Silas an arsonist as far back as the age of 5?

If he was, that would certainly complicate this case.

To say the very least.

## Chapter Eleven

AS I DROVE BACK from Fulton, I got on the phone with Anna. I would have to get Silas' mental health records. He had signed a release for me to get those records, because he knew I would have to get them. But as with the earlier issue, I wanted to get those records a lot faster, so I had Anna get them for me.

"I'll have them emailed to you by the time you get back to your office," she said.

I thought about what I found out from Silas' adoptive mother as well as his birth father. They were both painting a picture of somebody extremely troubled, to say the very least. His adoptive mother, Arlene, suspected him of crimes committed around the neighborhood. And his father, if he was speaking the truth, which was highly doubtful, but if he was speaking the truth, Silas had killed his own mother when he was only five years old. By setting a fire.

I had a feeling I would soon find out the truth. And that truth was that Silas was a violent person with an unhealthy obsession with fires, possibly suffering from pyromania, and who had no qualms about killing people in these fires. I mean, if he killed his own mother in a fire, why not also kill his wife in a fire? I also thought about the letter I received, about how the whole BDSM thing was just a cover for the fact that Silas apparently chained his wife to the wall so she would be helpless when he set the fire that killed her. How could I cast doubt on that letter? After all, when I went to see that dungeon, it really wasn't much of anything. I couldn't really tell if it was a dungeon ever, or if it was something else, like a guesthouse. I couldn't tell that. That bothered me.

I called Harper while I was driving.

"I wanted to give you an update on Silas," I said to her when she picked up. "Here's what I found out. I think my client is a psycho. A very intelligent psycho who happens to be fascinated with fire and who possibly killed his own mother in a fire when he was only five. He might have only been five at the time, but he was already in the third grade. And, apparently, he has at least one personality disorder, and that's attachment disorder. Right now, Anna is getting the records for me from Silas' stay in a mental hospital and I've a feeling that when I get those records I'm going to find out he has a lot more personality disorders than I even know about."

Harper was silent. "Damien, be careful. Please be careful. I know you deal with people who are seriously disturbed all the time, but that doesn't make me feel any safer. The worst kinds of people to deal with are the ones who combine personality disorders with high intelligence. If it's true he set a fire that killed his mother when he was only five years old, then he might be quite dangerous indeed. Just be careful."

"I'm not only going to be careful, but I think I better get

off the case." A part of me wanted to do that but another part of me didn't want to. After all, I was a criminal defense attorney. Harper was right. I dealt with people like Silas all the time. It was what I did. Granted, usually the people I dealt with did not have a genius level IQ and the power Silas had, but in my law career, I had dealt with my share of disturbed people. In fact, that was most of what I dealt with. So part of me wanted to keep going on this case and just be wary of anything he told me. If I found out he had been diagnosed with something such as narcissistic personality disorder or antisocial personality disorder, I would have to take that into account anytime he told me anything. Because if he had a severe personality disorder, most of what he would tell me would probably be lies.

"You can do what you want, nothing is stopping you," Harper said. "But I'm glad you're getting this information so at least you can know exactly what you're dealing with."

"Yes, that's true. Not to mention that when I find out this information, and I think Silas was guilty of murdering his wife, I can take the information and try to get a good plea deal for him." I didn't like to try a case when I knew for a fact my client was guilty. To me, trying a case with a client I knew to be guilty carried too much risk with it – such as the danger of getting the person acquitted, which inevitably meant that a dangerous person was back on the street. Of course, when dealing with clients such as Silas, there was always a fly in the ointment, namely that these clients often wouldn't take a plea deal. They usually couldn't be convinced about the danger they were in and would typically insist on a jury trial, come hell or high water. After all, people with severe personality disorders were used to getting their way with people. They had the intelligence and charm to snow almost anybody. They were only reasonable in thinking they could snow a jury just as well. Silas was probably just this kind of person, and he probably would never take a plea deal. That was a very real possibility and I had to face the facts.

I saw my office coming up, and I was anxious to see what Anna had come up with for me.

When I got to my office, the first thing I did was boot up my computer, and saw an email from Anna with an attachment.

"I'll call you back, Harper," I said. "I have to see what Anna sent me about Silas. I need to see for myself if my suspicions are true about him. After all, his adoptive parents are living hand to mouth in a very small house with very old furniture and very old carpeting and can barely make ends meet. Meanwhile, Silas is a billionaire. That alone tells me there's something wrong with him, that he would just allow his parents to live like that while he could easily give them enough cash to more than take care of them for the rest of their lives."

I hung up the phone, got on the computer and downloaded the attachment. In this attachment was reams and reams and reams of records from Silas' stay in the mental hospital. I saw he went into the hospital when he was 25 years old. This was after he'd started his company, but before it became public, which sent his net worth into the stratosphere. Apparently, according to his records, he was in the hospital for an entire year. That alone told me there were some very serious issues. It wasn't a simple stay in a mental hospital, where somebody might go into the hospital for a week while their meds get straightened out. No, this was something much worse.

The only thing that cheered me about what I was reading was the fact that Silas apparently had gone into the hospital of his own free will. That meant he knew he was having problems and was trying to deal with them. So that was one good thing. He had taken responsibility.

I read about what the psychologists and psychiatrists had made notes about him while he was in the hospital. While he was in the hospital, he was being treated for bipolar disorder, which apparently he really was suffering from. He had attempted suicide one week after he got into the hospital and his meds were changed at that time.

I started reading about some of the other symptoms he was exhibiting while in the hospital. Apparently, he had told the other patients that he was somebody whom everybody admired, and every woman wanted to be with him while every man wanted to be him. He told anybody who would listen that he would be president of the United States one day, and when he was, everybody would bend to his will.

This showed he thought a lot about himself, but then again, he was intelligent enough to do all of those things. He was smart enough to be president, as he had the drive to start his own company and make it an international concern grossing millions every single year. So, while the psychologist had decided he was exhibiting delusions of grandeur, it might've just been something else.

The psychologist also said he had noted that Silas had a lack of empathy for the people around him. He couldn't show the least bit of care for the other patients. For instance, somebody who he played cards with every day committed suicide, but Silas seemed to not care about that fact. He refused to go to the funeral and made comments about his friend like "He brought it on himself, so why should I care about what happened to him?" Apparently, this was not an isolated incident, as many of the people he acquainted himself with had issues that Silas walked away from. He simply couldn't put himself in their shoes.

After reading some of the other notes, I saw that the preliminary diagnosis for Silas was indeed narcissistic personality disorder. According to the notes, he had all the hallmarks of this kind of disorder. He would only talk about himself, never bothering to find out about anybody else around him. He believed he was superior to everybody around him, which, intelligence-wise, he probably was, but he apparently belittled everyone he knew. He would only focus on the flaws of others and never took responsibility for any of his own flaws. He also could not take any kind of criticism and was constantly looking for someone to validate him. In fact, if someone criticized him, he would fly into a rage, even if the criticism was small and minor. He also apparently felt entitled, in that he expected people around him to do everything for him and he never quite understood why they would not want to do things for him. Not only that, but he also apparently used people for his own means, and was also extremely envious of others.

In other words, it seemed he fit all the criteria of someone suffering from this kind of disorder.

I put my head on the desk. I was confused about what to do, yet I questioned why I was desiring to get off his case. He was paying me a lot of money. A lot of money I could use. So there was that. But I just didn't know if I was equipped to deal with somebody who quite possibly was a very dangerous person. Not that I didn't deal with dangerous people all the time. But there was something about this guy that just sent chills up and down my spine, and maybe question why I took the case in the first place. I just had a horrible feeling about him from the very beginning.

It turned out my gut was right. As it always was. I thought when I met him that he killed Ava. Granted, I had not yet worked out a motive for killing her, but if he was the kind of person I thought he was, it wouldn't take much to set him off. Perhaps she just pissed him off. Maybe she started out catering to his needs, but then decided to stop, and, just like that, he decided to kill her. I didn't know. What I did know was that the puzzle pieces were coming together, and it was becoming more and more clear that I was most likely dealing with a psycho.

As I was looking at the records, I looked up.

Silas Porter was standing in my doorway, and he was looking at me.

And he did not look happy. To say the very least.

## Chapter Twelve

"CAN I HELP YOU?" I asked him defensively. What was with this guy, always barging in like this? Seriously, did he think he was my one and only client?

He had that same inscrutable expression he had when he first met me. That expression that told me very little about what was going through his mind. "I wanted to check on what you found out about my case. Have you talked to the prosecutor?"

I shook my head. "No. Your case hasn't gone to the Grand Jury yet, so you have not been formally charged with anything. I know you were preliminarily charged, but you have to understand that the formal charges don't come until the Grand Jury reviews your case and decides whether there's enough evidence to bound you over for trial. That's how it works in this jurisdiction. So I don't think the permanent prosecutor has been assigned to your case yet. I will tell you that I've spoken with the temporary prosecutor, the one who handled the initial appearance on your case, and she told me that at the moment the only offer in your case is life in prison without the possibility of parole. I figured that this was probably something you didn't want to consider and—"

All at once, I saw fury in those light eyes. However, his voice was completely controlled. "Mr. Harrington, I thought I was clear. I will not entertain any kind of plea agreements in this case. I told you that my wife died before the fire had ever come in, and I think she died of natural causes. Now what did you find out about Ava and her health?"

"I found out she was perfectly healthy. I got her medical records, and there was nothing wrong with her. Her heart was fine. Everything checked out with her when she last got a physical. So I don't know what caused her to just die of natural causes, as you say she did."

He sat down. "Well, you're going to have to keep looking. Keep trying to figure out why my wife died like that."

I looked at him. I decided I would gauge the reaction to what I would say to him next. "I have put in a motion to have your wife's body exhumed. According to the preliminary autopsy, there wasn't any kind of traceable poison in her system, however I don't know if they would've been looking for that. I understand that her body was in such a state that's entirely possible they couldn't discover if there was poison in her tissues at all. However, I have to try. That's the only thing that makes sense to me. Somebody poisoned her. That's the reason she died."

I looked into those eyes and saw he was a bit perturbed by what I was saying. However, it didn't seem like he was totally opposed the idea. "Do you think I poisoned her?" he asked me.

"I don't know. Did you?"

He just stared at me. I had no idea what he was thinking, however I knew it probably wasn't good. "Do you think I'm capable of doing something like that?"

I thought about everything I had found out about him these past few days. About how his father said he set a fire that killed his mother when he was only five. About how his adoptive mother was living in such a state and he wasn't helping them out at all. About how his mother said she was happy to get him out the house when he was only 15, and how he ran away many times. And when he ran away, there were crimes that happened all over their neighborhood. I thought about what the psychologists at the mental institution, where he spent a year, wrote in their notes - he was suffering from narcissistic personality disorder. I thought about all those things.

However, I decided I not to say anything about any of those visits. Not yet. Something told me he probably already knew I made these visits. However, I wouldn't necessarily come out and say that to him. "Mr. Porter, I believe that anybody is capable of anything. If somebody pushes somebody's buttons just right, even the most mild-mannered person is capable of killing somebody. So yes, I do think you're capable of poisoning your wife."

He cocked his head. "If you think I did it, I killed my own wife, then why would you take my case?"

That question confused me, to say the very least. Did he not remember he pressured me to take his case? That he came into my office, and begged me to take his case, saying he only wanted me to be his attorney, and nobody else? Did he not remember that? I looked into his eyes and knew that of course he remembered that. It was obvious he did.

"Because that's what I do. I defend people whether or not they're guilty of what they did. I just need to know the truth. I need to know the truth because then I'll know if I'm going to try to plead you out or try the case. But since you're pretty adamant you're not going to plead this case out, then maybe I don't want to know the truth after all. Because, as you probably know, if I know you're guilty, I can't put you on the stand. Not if I know you're going to lie. But yes, I do think you are more than capable of killing your own wife."

He steepled his hands, still staring at me. He stared at me for what seemed like an eternity, but probably was only a few minutes. "And why, pray tell, would I have killed her? You know, that's been the one thing that nobody has ever been able to tell me. The prosecutors are convinced I have done this. However, nobody has told me why I would have wanted to have killed her. I'm sure you have not thought that through. I certainly didn't kill her for the money. After all, I have more than enough money myself. I don't need her millions. Is there any reason why I would've killed her?"

"I don't know." I knew I would have to find that out. In fact, the next place I would go to do my investigation would be Ava's parents. I had a feeling they would be very enlightening, and I had a feeling that after I talked to them, I would know exactly why he would've killed his own wife. Because Silas was correct about one thing – as of now, I didn't know what his motive was for murdering Ava. But when I spoke with Ava's parents, they would give me a fuller picture of what his relationship with Ava was like. Only when I found this out could I make a decision on whether or not I thought Silas killed her and why.

The only question in my mind at that point would be how he did it. Did he kill her by poisoning her or did he kill her with the fire? He was capable of killing somebody with a fire. Granted, he might've only been five years old when he possibly killed his own mother with a fire, but it showed what he was capable of.

"Okay," Silas said. "You do some more investigation. I know my case will go to the Grand Jury sometime soon. I also know nobody's ever certain when the Grand Jury convenes. It's a secret process, I know that. However, I also know they'll find enough evidence to charge me. So hopefully we'll soon know who'll be our trial judge and we can go from there. In the meantime, I need you to keep me in the loop. Don't shut me out. And when you do your investigation, I want to know who you speak with. It's very important to me that I can rebut any untruths people might say about me. Do you understand that?"

I nodded but said nothing. I knew I probably should've told him about all the people I've spoken with about him, but, at the same time, I knew that if he was suffering from narcissistic personality disorder that he was a good liar and would tell any lie possible to cover up his tracks. If I would've told him I'd spoken with his adoptive mother and his birth father and had gotten the records on his mental hospital stay, then he would have a story to counter all of them. I didn't want to hear his lies. I wanted to come up with my own version of the truth. I didn't want to be swayed. So I decided to keep quiet about what I was finding out about him.

Maybe that was not the best course of action. After all, he would have to find out sooner or later what evidence I had about him. But I wanted to fill in the missing puzzle pieces before I presented everything to him. That way I would be on more solid ground, and if he wanted to lie to me, I would at least have a better picture of the truth.

That was the only way I could handle his case. I certainly wouldn't present his case based upon his statement of the facts, because that would mean I would never know the truth.

## Chapter Thirteen

ON MONDAY, I filed a motion with the court to have Ava's body exhumed, and I knew I would have to ask the medical examiner to specifically look for some kind of poison. I didn't even know the state the body was in and if there was even enough left of Ava to test for poison. However, I knew I had to try.

The prosecutor did not object to the motion, so the judge signed the order, and I could have Ava's body exhumed from her grave. I wanted also to be present for the new autopsy.

So, two days later, I went to the Medical Examiner's Office. I was alerted that the autopsy would take place that afternoon. A prosecutor would also be there.

The prosecutor who came was not necessarily the person who would be the one trying the case. I knew that, but I was happy to see Ally Hughes anyways. I hoped she would be on the other side because we got along well. And, so far, we were hitting it off in the romance department. It complicated things slightly, but I knew that both of us were professional enough to get past our personal relationship and give this case our all.

"So what do you hope to find out about this?" Ally asked me. "When I got your motion, I was confused as to what you're looking for."

"I just wanted to find out if maybe something happened that was overlooked in the original autopsy."

"Well, from what I understand, the body was so badly burned I don't know if you'll find out anything new about her."

We walked into the room where the Medical Examiner was prepared to do a second autopsy on the body. When I saw the condition of the body, however, I knew there would be very little the medical examiner could find out about how Ava died. The poor woman was little more than a pile of charred bones. The only thing that was relatively intact were her fingers.

"Will you be able to tell me if there's a possibility that poison was found in Ava's system at the time she died?" I asked the medical examiner, whose name was Dr. Prorock.

"I'm afraid that might not be possible. As you can see, there is very little left to test in this body. All of her internal organs were burned in the fire, as was her skin, her blood, everything. I'll do what I can. However, if this was a poison that was hard to trace in an intact body, it might be impossible to trace in a body this badly burned."

I watched as the Medical Examiner looked around for something that would indicate Ava had been poisoned, however, after an hour, she shook her head. "I can send what's left of the tissue to pathology. However, I just don't know what pathology can tell me, or you for that matter. I'm afraid that if Mrs. Porter was poisoned before she died, there will probably be no way of telling it."

"What about her fingers?" I looked at the fingertips that were the only really intact part of her body. "Can you tell a thing from them?"

"Yes, that is useable tissue, so that is what I'll be sending to pathology. Also-"

"Also what?" I asked her.

She shook her head. "I suppose, in an abundance of caution, I should make an impression of the fingertips. I should get her fingerprints on file to go along with her dental records. I understand that the body has been positively identified by Mr. Porter, because he has stated this was his wife. At the same time, in situations like this, we can never be too careful." At that, she made an impression of Ava's fingerprints. "This will go with the dental records, just in case there's any question that this is Mrs. Ava Porter."

I thought that was probably overkill, considering the fact that Silas had been in the room when his wife died, therefore could positively identify her. But I also knew that as a medical examiner, she needed to make a good record. And, apparently, the first time she did the autopsy, she didn't make that record with her fingerprints. She did make a record with Ava's dental records, however. I knew the dental records were a close match for Ava, so that was another way of identifying her.

"Well, I found this little bit of tissue I could send to the pathologist, but, as I said, my guess is that the results will be inconclusive as to whether or not Mrs. Porter was poisoned," Dr. Prorock said.

"Thank you," I said.

Ally and I left the medical examiner's Office together. She smiled at me. "I guess I'll be seeing you later." She winked at me and shyly touched my leg with her shoe. I got her drift. She and I had a date on the weekend, and we both were looking forward to it. I planned on taking her to see a play at the Uptown Theater, followed by dinner on The Country Club Plaza.

"We'll have fun on our date," I said.

"We will."

## Chapter Fourteen

THE VERY NEXT day I went to see Ava's parents. I just knew they had information for me that could be more helpful than what anybody else had been able to tell me. After all, they knew the most about Ava's relationship with Silas. It sounded to me like Ava was close with them. I had a feeling Ava probably told her parents about their relationship, things that made them hate him. After all, I was finding out more and more reasons that Ava's parents would have him on their shit list. Not just because of his background but because of the person he was.

I had called them and they told me the best time to come over would be at 6 o'clock that evening. So I called Gretchen, my sitter, and told her I would be late coming home and to heat up leftovers for the kids' dinners. I didn't like to do that very often, but I knew this was a rare occasion, one I could not pass up. I had to find out for myself what kind of person I was dealing with.

I got to the Jacksons' house. Opal and Matthew Jackson lived in the Mission Hills area, the most exclusive area in the city. Unlike Hallbrook, however, this was an area that mainly housed people who came from old money. I knew that's what the Jackson's were – old money. Matthew Jackson was an heir to a shipping fortune. He was semiretired and was a billionaire in his own right. I also knew that Ava herself had been given millions of stock in her father's company when she turned 18.

The house was a Tudor structure situated behind a circle drive with a large fountain in the middle of it. As I approached the door, I looked up at the three stories. A small Asian maid opened the door and she bowed her head. "Mr. and Mrs. Jackson are expecting you," she said as she swept her hand towards the foyer. "Come, follow me. They are in the study."

I followed the maid through mazes of hallway until I finally got to the door which apparently led to the study. The maid lightly rapped on the door, which was answered by a woman who was probably in her 60s. She was dressed in a matching jacket and skirt, hose, pumps, and pearls. Her hair was preferably coiffed and her nails were perfectly manicured. She was slender, probably only weighing about 110 pounds, and she seemed to be fit. I could see her face was probably heavily worked on, however, so I didn't really know how old she was.

She smiled at me. "Come on in. We've been expecting you," she said pleasantly.

A very tall man with a full head of hair came over to me and extended his hand. He was wearing a sweater over his slacks and, like his wife, his hair was perfectly cut. "My name is Matthew Jackson, and I understand you are investigating the murder of our daughter, Ava."

"Yes. I am investigating what happened to her. And it's very important I speak with you, because I wanted to know what you know about Ava and her relationship with my client."

"Please, have a seat." Opal gestured to a large wingback chair. "What would you like to know about our daughter?"

"Well, I am most interested in what you know about her relationship with my client, Silas Porter."

She shook her head. "I know this will not surprise you, because I'm quite sure our son-in-law has told you how we feel about him. We never wanted our daughter to be with him. I know he says the reason why we never wanted her to be with him was because we didn't think he was good enough because he was poor at one time. I can tell you that nothing is further from the truth. If I thought for a second he had treated her the way she deserved to be treated, we would never object to their union. However, that was not the case. I can also tell you that at the time our daughter was murdered, she wanted to leave him. In fact, she had fallen in love with somebody else. His name is David Taylor. He's a golf pro who lives down the street. In fact, my husband take lessons from him. That's how Ava met him."

I suddenly knew that my client *did* have a motive for killing his wife. If it was true that his wife had met somebody else, and she was about to leave my client for this other person, then that would be his motive. Apparently, however, the prosecutors didn't yet know about this turn of events. At least, they hadn't been able to ascribe this motive to him. In fact, that was always the nagging fact in my head when I thought about this case. Because up until now, I didn't know why Silas would've killed Ava. Now I did. I knew, from representing abused women in custody cases, the most dangerous time in an abusive situation was when the abused spouse is about to leave her abuser. Silas must've known Ava had met somebody else and was ready to leave. If he did deliberately kill her, that would be why.

"David Taylor. Can I have his phone number? I need to speak with him. Something tells me he has information I'm going to need. In the meantime, what can you tell me about Ava's relationship with Silas?"

"Just a second. Let me go into the kitchen and write down David's information for you," Opal said. "In the meantime, Matthew can fill you in on what you need to know about Ava's relationship with Silas." At that, she got up from her chair and left.

I looked at Matthew, who was sitting quietly in his chair. "I despised that man. I still despise him. I'm not afraid to tell you that I have always been tempted to quietly find somebody who could take care of him. Not kill him, but to pay him to go away. Because there's one thing about him - he'll do anything for money. I know he has a lot of money, he has more money than even we have, but he always wants more. I have never met a man with a more bottomless pit of greed than him."

I wondered if Matthew simply wanted to pay him to go away, or if there was something else to it. I knew that sometimes parents, when they know their child was being abused, especially if they knew the child was endangered, would do anything to protect that child. Anything. Then again, I wouldn't question him on this. It really wasn't my business. However, if something happened and my client was acquitted, then it was entirely possible that Matthew would take matters into his own hands. People have killed for less.

"Why do you hate him so much?"

"Because Ava was always coming over here and telling us what kind of person he was. We saw the bruises. She tried to play like they came from some other source, but we knew the truth. I found out his background. I know what kind of person he is. He's not the kind of person who should have been with my daughter. So I was very relieved when she met David and told me she was in love with him. She told me she would seek a divorce from Silas, and I couldn't have been happier. At the same time, I was extremely worried that something would happen to her. I knew Silas was not the kind of guy who would go quietly. And I was right. I never wanted to be right, but I was."

I thought about what I would do if I was in his situation. What would I do if Amelia grew up and married somebody who I suspected was abusing her and I was afraid for her life? I couldn't imagine being in such a situation.

And as I looked at Matthew, I saw his eyes were haunted. Yet, I could also see another emotion behind them. I couldn't quite understand why I also saw he was happy. I could read his expression and I could see joy mixed in with the sadness.

I wondered what that was all about.

Maybe he was happy because his son-in-law would finally get his? I shook my head. I didn't think that was it. After all, there was a good chance I could get him off. That was my hope, anyhow. So why wasn't he treating me with contempt? After all, if Silas was acquitted, it would be because of my work. And then there would be no justice for Ava.

"Mr. Jackson," I began. "Is there anything else you need to tell me?"

He shook his head. "No. Why do you ask that question?"

"I just have a feeling. I have a feeling there's something you're holding back from me."

"No. There's nothing I'm holding back from you. I can

tell you that Ava's identical twin Emma is still alive, and she's hurting. She's hurting very much. As a family, of course we've been devastated. But we're carrying on for Emma. It's the living people who give me joy. There's a hole in my heart for Ava, of course, but I can see her every day in Emma's eyes and that's what makes me happy."

This was another piece of information I didn't know until now. I had no idea Ava had an identical twin. I wondered why Silas never told me about that? At the same time, I also had to wonder if that piece of information was significant somehow. I didn't really know how it would've been. "Where is Emma?" I asked Matthew.

"Now, I don't want you to jump to conclusions, but she's living with David Taylor."

"David Taylor, the golf pro that Ava was going to marry?" Now, that was weird. Ava had just died and her fiancé was already taking up with her identical twin sister?

"Yes, the same person. After Ava died, he leaned on us for emotional comfort. Emma was around, and she looks identical to Ava, so she and David grew close. David tried to explain to us that he wasn't looking for Emma to replace Ava, but I think we knew better. Still, David is a good person, and I know he can grow to love Emma for who she is one day, not just because she looks identical to the woman he really loves. I know it's an unconventional situation, and believe me, our friends think it's very strange, but who are we to judge? The heart wants what it wants, and apparently David's heart wants Emma."

I blinked. "Ava has been dead for less than a month. And now you're telling me the man she found love with, her fiancé, the man who she was going to leave my client for, he's already moved on with her identical twin?" For some reason, that piece of information was not sitting well with me at all. There was a nagging voice in the back of my mind that was telling me something was off about this whole situation.

At that point, Opal was back in the room. "I know Matthew has told you that David is now with Ava's sister," she said. "I don't want you to be judgmental about that. They were close friends before Ava died, and they just got closer after she passed. There's really nothing more to it than that."

"Are Emma and David serious?"

"Yes. In fact, they're engaged. They've announced their engagement and are to be married this fall at the country club."

This was the weirdest thing. Before I visited these people, I didn't even know Ava had an identical twin sister. Now I knew she had one, and that said identical twin sister was engaged to the man she was in love with, the man she had wanted to marry. Ava had been dead for less than a month, yet her sister was already engaged to David?

"What can you tell me about Emma?" I asked Opal. "I'm so sorry, it's just that the fact that Ava has an identical twin is new news to me, so I need to find out as much information about her as I possibly can."

Matthew looked at me suspiciously. "Why do you want information about Emma? What does she have anything to do with how Ava died? After all, that's why you're here. You're here to find information that will help you in your investigation of what happened that night, between our son-in-law and our daughter. I fail to see how Emma figures into your investigation at all."

To tell the truth, I didn't know myself why I wanted to know about Emma. I just thought it was strange that she would move in so quickly on Ava's love.

I also noticed that after I started questioning the parents about Emma, their expressions towards me changed. Opal was looking at me suspiciously and Matthew wasn't looking at me at all anymore.

I cleared my throat. I wanted to change the subject. There was just something about me talking about Emma that changed the atmosphere, in ways both subtle and not-so-subtle, and I wanted to get back on track with these people. "Do either of you know whether or not Ava was seeking any kind of medical treatment at the time she died?"

Opal shook her head and Matthew continued to look away from me. "No," she said uncertainly. "I would have known if Ava was sick or if she had any kind of life-threatening illness, but she never told me anything about that."

"Are you certain about that?"

"I am. What made you ask that question?"

I didn't quite know what to tell her. I knew why I wanted to know the answer to that, and that was because Silas insisted that Ava was dead before the fire swept in, but I also knew Opal and Matthew were not going to be hearing anything that might clear their son-in-law. It was pretty obvious that the two of them wanted him behind bars and I didn't really blame them for that. After all, as far as they knew, Silas was an abusive husband to their daughter. They would go to any lengths possible to protect her. Or, should I say they would go through any lengths possible to make sure Silas would be put behind bars so he couldn't prey on any other young woman. So they probably weren't the best people to ask about any kind of health issues that Ava might've had. Even if they knew she was dying, they would never tell me that, because that fact might have exonerated Silas.

"I'm just trying to cover all the bases. Now, is there anything else you want to tell me about the relationship Silas and Ava had? Anything at all?"

"No," Opal said. "We have told you everything we know about the two of them. Now I know you have a job to do, and your job is to try to make sure that monster is back on the street. I beg you not to do that. Do what you can to make sure he ends up in prison. I know I'm asking you something that is against all of your ethics. But you have to believe this, nobody belongs behind bars more than Silas Porter."

"Duly noted." I got up from the chair. "I'll let myself out. And I'm gonna go ahead and give a call to David Taylor."

I walked out of the house, and immediately got on the phone with David. He answered on the second ring. I told him what I needed, and he invited me to come over to his office and speak with him the next day. He explained to me that he would be working on paperwork at the country club in his office and would have time to see me tomorrow afternoon.

The next day, as I headed to David's office, I just had a feeling there was something I was missing. The answer to me should be obvious. However, I just couldn't figure it out right at that moment.

Maybe seeing David would help clear things up.

## Chapter Fifteen

THE NEXT DAY, I went to the Mission Hills Country Club, which was situated on a tree-filled lot a stone's throw away from the Jacksons' house. I went through the doors and was directed to David's office.

I knocked on the door to the office, and a tall and lean man with a mop of brown hair and green eyes stood up and greeted me. "Hello, you must be Damien. Come in, have a seat." He gestured to the chair in front of his desk.

I sat down as he sat casually across from me behind his desk. This man looked a lot more friendly than Silas ever did. Instead of the cold stare I always got from Silas, David had a warm look in his eyes. His expression was mirthful and he seemed very relaxed. I was struck by how different he was from Silas, which was probably what Ava was looking for.

"Now, what can I do for you?" he asked.

I got out my pad of paper and pen. "As I told you over the phone, I'm the lawyer for Silas Porter. I appreciate you answering my questions, because I'm trying to get to the bottom of what happened between Silas and Ava."

"Shoot," he said. "Ask away. I'm happy to help."

It was slightly peculiar that he was so open and willing to help me. After all, I was investigating the murder of his girlfriend, and I was representing her alleged murderer. If I was in David's shoes, I certainly would not be as affable or friendly as this guy was.

"Now I understand you and Ava were having an affair. Is that right?"

"Yes. And, to tell you the truth, I think that was probably why Silas killed her. She was always telling me how scared she was of Silas. I was urging her to leave him because I wanted to marry her. I wanted to provide a life for her. But she told me that if she left him, he would kill her. In fact, he had told her over and over again that he would kill her if she left him. And I'm not surprised about the way he killed her. He's just the kind of person who would want someone who he was angry with to die an agonizing death. It wouldn't be enough for him to smother her with a pillow, or slip something into her drink, or something like that. He would want her to suffer. So when I found out that Silas had killed my girlfriend in such a way, I wasn't surprised."

I studied him. Here he was, talking about the fact that his girlfriend was murdered, burned alive, and he didn't seem to have any kind of emotion about that fact. In fact, he was smiling.

I always was a careful study of people's expressions and emotions, which was how I could pick a jury as well I did. The body language, the facial expressions, everything – these are all things that would belie how a person was really feeling. The words coming out of David's mouth were angry words, but he didn't have the right expressions or posture to back up those words. He didn't seem to be angry to me, no matter how angry his words were.

I wondered if he was the kind of guy who didn't really get angry. Maybe he was just one of those happy-go-lucky guys who could talk about the burning death of his girlfriend with a gleam in his eye.

"So when Ava told you she was afraid of Silas, she was afraid he would kill her, how did you react to that? Did you help her get a restraining order or anything like that?"

I knew the answer to that. There were no restraining orders against Silas. There were, years before, but there were none recently.

"No. We thought it was pretty pointless. After all, you could have a restraining order against somebody, but if that person breaks that restraining order, what can you really do? I mean, I know you can have the person arrested and thrown in jail, but Silas is a very powerful man, and we knew that there would be no way he would ever be deterred by a restraining order." He was still relaxed when he said this. He was leaned back in his chair with one leg crossed over the other at the knee and his elbow was on his desk.

"I guess I don't really understand. It takes so little time to execute a restraining order. It's literally a matter of filling out a form, filing it, then showing up to court. In fact, you could even get what's called an *ex parte* order without even going to court. And you're wrong about one thing – if there was a restraining order, then the second he sets foot on her property, he would go to jail. Even before he did anything threatening. So it's worth the extra steps to get that order, isn't it?" If he loved her, then that's what he would've done. If he loved her, he probably would have done all he could to make sure she was safe. It seemed like he did very little, maybe nothing.

He shrugged his shoulders. "I guess I just didn't see a need for it."

"What did you do to protect her? Did you urge her to take any self-defense classes, or show her how to use a gun? Assuming you know how to use a gun yourself. Did you hire a bodyguard for her? Install an alarm system for her? Did you have her move in with you, and make sure there was protection for her? I guess I need to find out from you what steps you took to make sure Ava was safe from Silas."

For the first time, he started to seem uncomfortable to me. His eyes flew towards the window, and then he looked down at his desk. I was finally beginning to see some sense of agitation in his body language, but surprisingly enough, it was because I was questioning him, and not because he was upset about the situation with Ava. "I guess I didn't do anything to protect her. I guess maybe I should have."

What an odd response. Damn right, he should have. I looked to see if there was any sense of remorse he had, but I saw there was none.

"Now, from what I understand, you're now living with her identical twin sister, Emma. Is that right?"

"Yes. After Ava passed away, Emma became my rock. It was during the lowest part of my life, and she and I were always good friends to begin with. You have to understand that I've known the family for years. I've given the Jacksons golf lessons since I became a pro. But before that, I knew them from the country club. I've been a member of this country club since I was a young boy, so I grew up with all of them. After Ava died, Emma told me she'd always had a crush on me, and it just kinda happened. Surely you don't begrudge me for having a new love in my life, do you?

"No, of course I don't begrudge you. I'm just gathering information." To tell the truth, I was trying to get information from him, but I wasn't exactly clear what kind of information I was looking for. "Now, I'm going to ask the same question I asked Ava's parents. Was she sick? Was she seeing a doctor for any reason?"

David shook his head. "No, she wasn't sick." That was all he said about that, however, and he answered a bit too quickly for my taste. He didn't try to ask me why I asked that question. He didn't look askance. He didn't pause. It was as if he knew that question was coming. "Is there anything else I can do for you?" he asked. "I don't want to be rude, but I have some new clients coming this afternoon. In fact, they're going to be here in the next 10 minutes, and I have to meet them on the course. So, if there's anything else, I can certainly make an appointment for you to come in again." His demeanor was back to being pleasant, affable and friendly.

"No. At the moment, I don't think that any follow-up will be necessary. However, I thank you for the open invitation. You're right, there might be something that might come up in the near future, and then I'll have to come back here and ask you some more questions. But, at the moment, I don't really have anything else for you."

I walked away from David's office thinking I was no closer to figuring out the story than I was before. On the one hand, David confirmed to me that Ava was afraid of Silas, and he also supplied the added detail that she was specifically afraid he would kill her in a painful way, because that was the way Silas was. If he's enraged, he's going to make you suffer. On the other hand, David's demeanor was just so off for the situation. Something wasn't right with him.

I got out onto the street and decided to turn right back into his office. I knew David would be on his way out, but hopefully I could catch him. I had just one more question for him.

I caught him as he was coming out of his door. "I see you're back," he said with a smile. "Was there anything else you need to ask me?"

"Yes. A question just occurred to me. Do you happen to know anything about Silas's background?"

"What do you mean by that? What specifically are you asking me?"

"I'm asking you if you know how his mother died?"

"Yes. I know. She was killed in a fire, and there was a great deal of suspicion that Silas might have started it. I don't know how that's even possible, considering the fact he was only five years old at the time, but Ava told me he was always fascinated with fire. She's always told me she suspected him of setting fires around the neighborhood where he used to grow up. She also told me she wouldn't be surprised to find out he's starting fires even now as an adult. She said he talked about it all the time – starting fires now. He played it off as a joke. But Ava was afraid it really wasn't a joke, and he would one day end up pushing her into a campfire when they go camping. That's another reason why I wasn't surprised Silas killed her in such a way."

Again, he was talking nonchalantly about the love of his life burning to death. So. Odd.

I cocked my head. There was another question I needed to ask, but the reason why I would ask this question was unknown to me even at that time. But for some reason, I felt it was relevant. "Is your father a doctor, by any chance?"

"Yes. He is. He's a PhD chemist, working for the federal government. Why do you ask?"

"No reason." And that was true at that moment. I didn't really have a reason for asking him if his father was a doctor. So his father was a doctor, so what? He wouldn't poison his own wife. I mean his own fiancé. He would have no reason to have poisoned Ava.

Would he have?

## Chapter Sixteen

AS I LEFT the country club, I was filled with questions. It seemed that meeting David had unsettled me, even more than meeting Silas did. What was up with that? I mean, the way he spoke with me about the love of his life being burned to death - it was as if he was talking about going shopping at a grocery store that day. Picking up his dry cleaning. Helping one of his clients. He certainly did not have the emotional demeanor of somebody whose love was killed in such a manner. And what was up with him not doing anything to protect her? According to him, Ava had told him she was afraid of Silas, and she thought he was dangerous and fascinated with fire. Knowing all that, and he did nothing to make sure she was safe? That did not sit well with me at all. Not at all.

I decided to go to my office, so I could decompress and think about what was going on with David. I called Gretchen to watch the kids. She lived only a few houses down and was usually available. If she wasn't available, then I probably would've went home.

She was available and happy to visit with Nate and Amelia until I could make it home. I was grateful for that. I really needed to be alone with my thoughts. I was so close to figuring out exactly what happened between Silas and Ava, and I just needed to be in the quiet and concentrate. That was most important to me at that moment.

But I got into the office and saw a familiar person sitting on the couch.

"Hello, Sargis," I said to Sargis Gregorian. He was an Armenian mobster that Harper knew from working on a case in Los Angeles a few years back. Since then, he had come to visit Harper and me from time to time, and, surprisingly, neither of us dreaded his visits. I knew he was a cold-blooded killer, as he was a mobster and that was what mobsters do, but in my job I knew so many cold-blooded killers that it didn't creep me out to be around him. And he was a surprisingly affable and cultured man. He was the kind of guy I could picture sitting in a wood-paneled room by the fire, calmly sipping a glass of scotch while he read Proust and listened to Beethoven. He was well spoken and extremely intelligent.

"Hello, Damien." He usually addressed me as Mr. Harrington, but just recently he had taken to referring to me by my first name. I guessed that meant we were on a first-name basis, so to speak. "And should I say, good evening?"

I sat down. "So what brings you here?"

"I was just going to check on you. I wanted to see how things are going with your new case. You have to understand, Silas is a close personal friend of mine. When he was accused of murder, he called me, and I informed him you were the best attorney they could possibly get for this case. I really do believe that Silas' case will do wonders for your career."

I narrowed my eyes. "Oh. So you're the reason why Silas was so adamant about hiring me. Is that right?"

"Yes. I definitely insisted you are the best person for this job, because I know you'll get to the bottom of what happened here. I have my suspicions. I'm sure you do too. But I have faith in you, faith you will get past the falseness of what everybody believes about what happened and get to the truth."

I was surprised that Silas had a connection to Sargis, but I probably should not have been. After all, Silas was an international businessman who headquartered his firm out of Silicon Valley. Sargis was part of a family that ruled Southern California. I should not have been surprised their paths might've crossed a time or two. But I did wonder if there was any kind of business arrangement the two of them had. Was Silas somehow involved with the mob? And if he was, so what? Perhaps Ava had somehow run afoul of the Gregorian clan, and Silas was hired to murder her? Was Sargis here to get me to go down a different path than the one I was going down before?

"What suspicions do you have about the situation?" I asked him.

At that, he brought out a file. "Here are the medical records you seek. I understand Silas was concerned that maybe Ava had some undisclosed health issues which would cause her to have died so suddenly. But these are the records not for Ava, for she was very healthy, but for her identical twin sister, Emma. I think you will find these records enlightening, to say the very least."

I looked at Sargis' face and I wondered why he'd gone

through the trouble of getting Emma's records. "I don't understand."

"Oh, I think you do." At that, he stood up. "Well, I must be on my way. I have a meeting with Erik. As you are probably aware, I come to Kansas City from time to time to see how the Kansas City division of our clan is faring." He smiled. "As much as I enjoy visiting you and Harper, you mustn't think I made a special trip just to see the two of you. Although that might not be a bad idea one day."

In spite of myself, I smiled as well. "Take care of yourself, Sargis."

He tapped his forehead. "The answer is there. You just have to put the pieces together. And I hope these records will help you do that." He turned to walk towards the door and then he turned back. "I know Silas well. I know he's had a lot of issues in his youth, but a murderer, he is not. I hope you realize that."

And then he turned and left.

## Chapter Seventeen

I SHOOK my head after Sargis left. It was so odd he would stop in like that and just dump these records on me.

But as I read the medical records, I suddenly knew what he was getting at.

Maybe.

Emma Jackson, according to these records, was suffering from pancreatic cancer.

I stared at the diagnosis sheet. I knew something about pancreatic cancer. In most cases, it was a death sentence, and there was very little that could be done about it. Mainly it was because pancreatic cancer was considered to be what was called the "silent killer," in that the typical person does not show symptoms of the disease until was too far gone. The lifespan of a person diagnosed with pancreatic cancer was usually less than a year. Commonly, it was only a few months. That was the fate of a childhood friend of mine who contracted the disease when she was only 33 years old. She was diagnosed in February and died in April. Her story was extremely common with people suffering from this disease.

And yet... David Taylor was planning his wedding with her. Her parents never said a word about her illness. David certainly never said a word about her illness either. It seemed like that was something they would have brought up to me, especially when I was asking about whether or not Ava had any health issues.

I tapped a pen on my desk, thinking about this. The answer was right there in these medical records.

It was there. But what was it? Emma was desperately sick. So what?

I got on the phone. I called Opal Jackson and she picked up on the first ring.

"I was wondering if you would mind if I could speak with your other daughter, Emma. There's a few questions I needed to ask her about what she knew about Ava and Silas. Do you think it would be possible to speak with her?"

Opal was quiet for a few minutes. She finally spoke. "I suppose that could be arranged. Do you want her to come into your office or do you want to come here and see her? She's currently living with David. They live in a house on Ward Parkway by the Country Club Plaza. I understand your office is on the Country Club Plaza, so if you want to go visit her you certainly can or she can come to you."

I certainly wouldn't tell Opal I knew the truth about Emma's health. If Opal knew I knew the truth, then something told me she would not be so accommodating. In fact, David and Ava's parents were being far too accommodating about all of this. It seemed as if they were all bending over backwards to make sure I was given information I needed. They all but bent over backwards to tell me a story in lockstep with one another.

"That would be helpful if she could come to my office. Does she work? I mean, work outside the home. If she doesn't, I would appreciate it if she could come over to my office tomorrow at two." I had court appearances and depositions tomorrow morning, so the afternoon would be the earliest I could see her.

"I'll arrange it and call you if there are any changes."

"Thanks."

I got off the phone and read the medical records some more. It was definite that, according to these records, Emma did not have much time left. She was diagnosed some three months back, in April of this year.

Apparently, she was not feeling well for a matter of months. When she went to see her doctor, she explained that her lower back was hurting and her urine was very dark. She was also concerned that her feces were very light. Those were sure signs of liver blockage. She also had been losing weight and the doctor noticed she was slightly jaundiced. According to the notes, Emma had been to the doctor several other times before this particular visit and nobody had ever found anything wrong with her. It was suspected she had a gallbladder problem, and kidney stones were also a diagnosis given to her. But, apparently after doing a battery of tests, the doctors found out she had pancreatic cancer.

I read further. I saw she had elected not to do chemotherapy. According to the notes, she stated she had seen people on chemotherapy and that was not the route she wanted to take. According to the notes, her doctor had explained to her she had only between four and six months to live. She could have prolonged her life to up to a year if she did the chemotherapy.

In other words, Emma was terminal and she knew it.

So she had been diagnosed three months prior to this. I wondered who I would see the next day. Was I going to see a woman on death's door, and, if so, how come nobody said a word about that?

I thought about the fact that Sargis had brought me these medical records. If he didn't, there would be no way I would've ever found out Emma was dying of cancer. There would be no reason for me to have gotten these records. Legally, I knew the HIPAA laws were sacrosanct. It was very difficult to get information on a person's health, even in the best of circumstances. If Emma was relevant to the case, then I could've subpoenaed these records, but, at the moment, she wasn't legally relevant to the case. So if Sargis didn't bring these records to me, the fact that Emma was sick, no, dying, would have been unknown to me.

Completely unknown to me.

I then called Silas. "Silas," I said to him. "I would like to ask you a few questions."

"Certainly. What questions do you have for me?"

"Did you know Ava's identical twin sister, Emma?"

He was quiet for a second or two. "No, I didn't even realize Ava had an identical twin sister. Why do you ask that question?"

"Ava never talked about her twin sister?"

"As I said, I didn't realize she had a twin sister, so no, she obviously never talked about her."

Now that was extremely odd to me. Silas and Ava were married for seven years, and Ava never once talked about her sister? Granted, Ava and Silas lived in Silicon Valley, but they still maintained a house right here in the Kansas City area, close to Ava's parents. He knew her parents. Why did he not know she had an identical twin sister?

Very peculiar. But I knew I would have to ask Emma about her relationship with Ava.

"What made you ask that question?" Silas asked again. "That question didn't just come of the blue, did it?"

"No. It didn't. Listen, Silas, I need to get off the phone right now. I need to get ready to prepare for speaking with Emma tomorrow. She's coming into my office."

It seemed as if the possibility was strong that Ava and Emma were not on good terms. For whatever reason. After all, why would Ava not even tell Silas at all about the existence of an identical twin sister? That just didn't make any sense to me.

I got off the phone and shut down my computer. I would have to quit for the evening. I wanted to get home to the kids, and, besides, I needed some rest. I knew my subconscious had the overall answer to my questions. That was always the way it was with me – somewhere, in my heart, I always knew the answer. It was just a matter of my brain catching up with my heart.

And I had a feeling this would happen soon.

## Chapter Eighteen

THE NEXT DAY, Emma came into my office. I was struck by how fit she looked. She was tanned and muscular. She looked like one of those women who lived a life of leisure, so all they did all day was lay out by the pool and lift weights at the gym. She probably was a runner in her spare time. That was the kind of physique she had. She was blonde with her hair cut in a short bob, and she evidently just had her nails done. They were elegant, painted in white, while her toes were displayed in a peep toe pair of pumps that showed off her bright red toenails.

She was carrying a Louis Vuitton bag, in black, and was wearing a white dress. I knew something about Louis Vuitton items, because Sarah always bought them, paying $1,000 and up for a purse. We used to fight about her buying those Louis Vuitton bags all the time. Emma's white dress hugged her curves and I could see the outline of well-toned abs underneath the dress. Her legs, which were showed off by the shortness of the dress, were also muscular.

No doubt about it. Emma did not appear to be a woman on death's door. In fact, she looked extremely healthy.

I made a note to myself to ask Silas a few questions about Ava. I was starting to understand exactly what happened, but I didn't quite understand *why* it happened. That was the only thing rolling around in my brain.

"Hello, Mr. Harrington," Emma said, as she came into my office. "You wanted to see me? You want to ask me some questions about my sister?" She shook her head and wiped her eyes. "You have to excuse me, but I'm still so sad about losing Ava. My identical twin sister. You know, you always read about how identical twins have a psychic connection to one another? How if one twin hurts, the other one hurts just as much? Well, that's not just a myth. That's absolutely true. And when I lost my twin sister, it was as if I'd lost the other part of myself. Like half of myself was missing. So I know you're representing her killer, but I was hoping you could find your way towards seeing he take some kind of plea deal. I really don't want the case to go to trial and see the jury possibly acquit him. He deserves to go to prison for what he did to my sister. And I hope he rots there."

I studied her face. I was still trying to see any kind of indication she was sick, but there was just nothing. She looked, for all the world, like somebody who could leave my office and run a marathon. Hell, she probably did run marathons. At least, from the looks of her, she did.

"So you tell me you're very sad you lost your identical twin sister. Yet, Silas never even knew Ava had an identical twin sister. I find that very disconcerting. After all, Silas knew Ava's parents. Yet he never knew about you. Why would that be?"

She dabbed her eyes with a Kleenex. "Well, here's the

thing. My sister and I have always had a rivalry between each other. She was always stealing my boyfriends and vice-versa. I guess she just didn't want me to meet her husband. She was afraid I would steal him as well. But that didn't mean we weren't close. That we didn't love each other. It just meant we tried not to bring one another around when a guy we were interested in was also around. I don't know if that makes sense to you, but that's how it was between the two of us."

That really wasn't making sense to me. "With all due respect, Ms. Jackson, I don't really understand what you're saying. Yes, I can understand you were wary about Ava meeting men you're interested in and it was the same way for her. But Ava was married to this man for seven years. You mean to tell me you didn't attend her wedding? You never came to family gatherings?"

She assumed a defensive posture as I was talking her. She crossed her arms in front of her, she narrowed her eyes at me in a scowl, and she pursed her lips. I could tell I had struck a nerve. "Okay. I guess you've probably already figured out my sister and I were not close at all." And she looked away.

I cocked my head at her. "Oh. So you're telling me that what you were saying earlier about how you feel like you've lost a part of yourself, how you feel a psychic connection with your twin sister, and all of that – that was all a lie."

The sweet, prim, proper and grieving girl disappeared in front of my eyes. In her place was a hellion bent on revenge. "I wasn't aware I was on trial here. In fact, I think it's your client on trial. It's your client who will burn in hell for what he did. I know I wasn't all that close with Ava, but you have to understand she was still my sister. She was still my blood. She and I shared a womb."

"You shared a womb. Did you also share a man?" I was referring, in this instance, to David, and she knew it.

She stood up. "I don't have to take this from you. David and I are in love. But we were not dating at all while my sister was alive. We were just friends. Not that that's any of your business."

"I —" I would say something snarky to her, like how could she become engaged to the man her sister was engaged to, not even a month after her sister was murdered, but I did not want to antagonize her any further. There was no need for me to, really.

I wanted, for all the world, to ask her about her health issues. How she could look so hale and hearty when she was on death's door. But the last thing I wanted to do was attract a lawsuit from her for violating her privacy. For violating the HIPAA law. She seemed like the kind of person who would drag me into court for that so I decided to let that go.

I made a note to put Emma on my list of witnesses. There was something about her. And I couldn't quite put my finger on it. I felt slightly stupid for not putting that missing puzzle piece together but it was right there. Right there where I could almost touch it.

"Is there anything else you need to ask me, Mr. Harrington?" Emma asked me curtly. "If not, I have places I need to be." She looked at her nails. "I have a manicurist appointment in a half-hour. So, if there's nothing else…"

I shook my head. "No, at the moment there's nothing else. But I'll be sure and let you know if I have anything else for you."

"I'm sure you will." At that, she gathered up her bag and left my office without a word.

I doodled on my pad of paper as I thought about everything I was finding out in these past few days. My client was a narcissist, his father was schizophrenic. At the same time, I just had this feeling that the fact my client was narcissistic and had mental illness genes were not really relevant to this entire case. I just didn't know why, but there was something else out there. I just had to figure it out.

It was then that I got a phone call from the medical examiner's office. "Hello, this is Dr. Prorock from the Medical Examiner's Office. May I speak with Mr. Harrington?"

"This is."

"I wanted to call you with the preliminary results of our second autopsy on Mrs. Porter."

My heart started to race. The fact that the medical examiner was calling me was a good sign. It was my experience that if they didn't find anything, they probably would not call me but would send me a letter. "Thank you for calling me. What were your preliminary results?"

"We were able to test just enough of her tissue to find trace elements of a barbiturate called Secobarbital."

Secobarbital. Curiouser and curiouser. On the one hand, that made me feel better about the whole situation. Silas was probably correct when he said his wife was dead before the fire swept in. That meant she possibly did not burn to death in an agonizing fashion. Yet, at the same time, it put more of a question in my mind. Could Silas have done this to Ava?

Or maybe somebody gave her the barbiturate? But why?

And who?

"Thank you very much for calling me, Dr. Prorock. I appreciate your keeping me in the loop with this."

"You're welcome. If you don't need anything else, I'll be

getting back to my work. But please call me if you have any other questions. At any rate, I'm sure I'll see you at trial."

"I'm sure you will." I hung up the phone and I immediately started doing my research on Secobarbital. The research showed it was a barbiturate that typically was used to help people die in assisted suicide. But unless the medical examiner was looking for it, she probably wouldn't have found it in this case because of the condition of Ava's body.

I just didn't know if this new piece of information helped my case or hurt it.

It was then that I remembered another piece of information. David's father was a chemist. He worked for the government. Was that piece of information important? Why would David want to kill his own girlfriend? Maybe because he wanted to be with her sister?

I shook my head. It was something else. Some other reason why David or somebody around him would want to murder Ava.

I picked up the phone and called that medical examiner back. "Can you do me a favor?" I asked Dr. Prorock.

"Of course. What do you need?"

"Could you please do another round of testing on Ava's dental records? And, while you're at it, can you also send me a copy of the fingerprints? I have a hunch. I don't quite know why I have this hunch, but I do. Could you do those things for me?"

"I'll do those things today."

"Thank you."

As I banged my pen on the desk, I thought about what I was considering in my mind. It was a long shot, to be sure. But something told me I might, for the first time, be on the right track.

I guessed I would find out in a matter of hours.

## Chapter Nineteen

IN THE MEANTIME, I called Silas into my office. I might as well. Gretchen was home with the kids and I was determined to make a break in this case. There was a kernel in my brain, a kernel about what had really happened, and finding out if the person who died in that dungeon was actually Ava Porter, or, as I was starting to suspect, Emma Jackson, it was a first step towards trying to figure out what really happened.

Silas appeared in my office within the hour. "You wanted to see me?"

I tried to ignore the chill going up and down my spine when I looked at this man. I knew the reason why he gave me the creeps was because of what I found out about him being a narcissist. Somebody who quite possibly killed his own mother at the age of five. I would try to put all of that aside and ask him what I needed to ask him.

"I wanted to ask you about your wife. Now you told me earlier you had been away in Europe for six months before the incident happened. When you saw Ava for the first time after you got back, did anything strike you about the way she looked?" I thought about the woman in my office. The fit woman with the muscular body, killer abs and runner's legs. The woman with the ramrod straight posture and absolutely no sign of jaundice.

"I'm not sure what you're asking me?"

"Did she look the same as when you left for Europe? Was there anything different about the way she looked when you came home from Europe?"

"Yes. As a matter fact, she looked like she lost a lot of weight. That's why I thought she was sick. That and the fact that she suddenly died while we were intimate. But yes, I was concerned that she was having health problems."

"Besides the fact she looked like she had lost weight, was there anything else that concerned you about the way she looked?" I was trying to see if he noticed she was jaundiced.

"I did notice her skin was a different color. I don't know, she just didn't look as healthy as she did. I asked her several times if she was seeing a doctor for any issues, and she insisted she was not. She told me she was fine and healthy. I believed her. I mean, she looked like she lost weight and wasn't looking quite as healthy as she did, but if she told me she wasn't having health problems, I had no reason not to believe her."

I bit my lower lip. I would have to possibly make a motion to the judge to order Emma to give me a copy of her fingerprints. However, I hoped the medical examiner would call me with the results of the second round of dental records testing. While I knew that identical twins sometimes had very similar dental records, they were not always definitively identical. They usually had slight variations from one another. Identical twins also had different fingerprints. However, they also shared the exact same DNA. The dental records might be the definitive way to tell if the person killed in that room was Ava or Emma.

If it was Emma, why was she murdered? Why would she have traded places with her sister? That didn't make sense to me. I would have to really think on that one.

"Is it possible your wife was jaundiced?"

"I suppose it's possible. Her skin wasn't that yellow though. It was just... a different color. But, she explained to me she had gone to the spray tanning booth, which was why she was slightly more golden than the last time I had seen her. I had no reason not to believe that. I had no reason to question her. What's with all these questions?"

"Is it possible that the person in your dungeon at the time of death was not Ava, but Emma?"

He looked dumb-founded. He furrowed his brow and then looked down at the desk, putting his hand underneath his chin. He looked up at me. "I guess so," he said unsurely. "I'm very sorry for my reaction, but I'm still getting used to the fact that my wife had an identical twin she never told me about. That's still very odd to me."

I thought about my visit to the Jacksons. They clearly told me Emma and David grew up together and that the two of them were good friends before Ava's death. That would imply that Emma lived in town. Yet, if that were true, and Emma did live in town, that didn't make any sense to me. If she lived in town, surely Silas would have known her somehow. How hard would it be to keep an identical twin under wraps? That is if the identical twin lived in town.

"Just a second." I got out her medical records file. I needed to look closer on where the records originated from. I didn't pay much attention to that detail before - I had just glanced at the diagnosis, the doctors' notes and so forth. It was then I saw it – Emma was being treated at The Mayo Clinic, in Rochester, Minnesota. Not that that told me anything – it certainly didn't tell me whether or not Emma had lived in town at the time Silas and Ava were married. After all, the Mayo Clinic was world renowned. It was possible she would've gone to the Mayo Clinic no matter where she lived. Yet it also did not definitively answer for me that Emma was local, either.

And if Emma did not live in town, and was estranged from her sister, it would follow that it was doubtful Emma and David were friends for years. It would follow that David, and the Jacksons, were lying about all of it.

Why would they do that?

"Emma was being treated at the Mayo Clinic in Minnesota, as she was dying of pancreatic cancer. In fact, according to her medical records, she had only a few months to live and was diagnosed three months ago. That would mean that by the time you got back from Europe, assuming that somehow, someway, Emma took Ava's place, she would have been very, very sick. As you say, your wife had lost a lot of weight and her skin color looked different. She conveniently went in for a spray tan the day you came back. I would imagine she did because she wanted to cover up the fact that her skin was yellow. That would be my guess."

Silas was looking at me with a bit of a dumbfounded look. "I'm sorry. It's just I'm trying to process all this information. Are you telling me that my wife's identical twin sister, an identical sister I never knew about, was the one in my house when I came home from Europe? The identical twin was the one who I was intimate with? The identical twin died in that dungeon?" He shook his head. "But why? And who would've killed her?"

I tapped my finger on the desk. "I'm not real clear about any of it. But I can tell you one thing – if my theory is true, I'm gonna get to the bottom of what happened. I have a feeling that when everything is said and done, I'll be hanging quite a few people out to dry. Now I don't really see the motivation for any of this, although I have my suspicions. The only thing is, I hope I can prove it in a court of law. I'll have a problem getting Ava, who's posing as Emma, to give me her fingerprints. In fact, she probably won't. I can make a motion onto the court to ask her to do so, but if the judge says no, it could be very difficult to prove that Emma died, not Ava. That is unless the doctor can identify the dental records and can tell me definitively if the person burned in that house was Emma."

I wasn't even sure if the dental records would definitively prove who was who. They were identical twins, after all. Identical twins often had different dental records, but it was also possible that the dental records were similar enough that the doctor couldn't make a definitive judgment about it. If that was the case, I would have a hard time proving what I had to prove. I could prove it by circumstantial evidence – the fact that the person posing as Emma would be coming into court, healthy and hearty. However, there was no way I could use her medical records against her, so how would I could I show the jury that Emma was supposed to be extremely sick? I would have to legitimately have possessed Emma's medical records, but there was no way I could legally subpoena them because she wasn't a party to the case. And there would be a problem showing a judge why I needed those records. My theory was so farfetched, I just didn't know if I could get a judge to sign off on me legally subpoenaing the medical records, and legally asking "Emma" to give me her fingerprints.

I would just have to try. Hopefully the dental records would be sufficient, but if they weren't, I would be facing an uphill battle.

An uphill battle, but not impossible. Nothing was impossible. And I faced longer odds before.

"I'm waiting on results of the dental record test. I'm assuming both Ava and Emma have seen dentists during their lifetime, so hopefully that will give me the answer I'm looking for."

Hopefully. Without it, I would be pushing a boulder uphill.

## Chapter Twenty

I GOT the results back from the Medical Examiner. My hunch was right. The person who died in that dungeon was not, in fact, Ava Porter. Now it was just a matter of proving who she really was.

Unfortunately, Ava, or at least a woman I assumed to be Ava, was not making things easy. I filed a motion with the judge because I needed a copy of her dental records or fingerprints. Either one. I knew I could always ask Anna to get a copy of Ava's dental records, however I needed to do something aboveboard this time. Otherwise, there was no way I could ever get the records into court.

Judge Pruitt was the judge assigned to this case. He was a no-nonsense judge. Ally Hughes was on the other side of the case. I was happy to see that, because Ally and I were in a good place, as far as our relationship went. We didn't see each other a lot, because both of us were immersed in this case, but we certainly were getting along well.

I got into the courtroom and waited for Harper to appear. I saw that Ava herself, or the woman I assumed to be Ava, was already sitting in the gallery. She was with her parents and looked good and healthy, just like the day she came into my office. I didn't have any sympathy for her.

Did she really think this kind of thing would work?

Of course, I didn't quite know what it would take to prove to the court that Emma was actually Ava. If I could just prove that, I would certainly be on the road to formally proving my theory. It was shaping up to be a good theory I could bring into the court and hopefully convince a jury.

Judge Pruitt took the bench. "Counselor," he said to me. "I understand you have a motion on file to examine the dental records and fingerprints of a party who is not even a part of this case. Is that true?"

I approached the bench and so did Ally. "Yes, as is indicated in my motion, the medical examiner has determined the person killed in my client's home was not Ava Porter. She has an identical twin, her name is Emma, and the person who has been pretending to be Emma is in this courtroom right now." I motioned over to Ava, sitting in the gallery with a pissed-off look on her face. "I submit to you that the person in this gallery is the alleged victim, Ava Porter. However, I need to prove it."

Judge Pruitt looked over at Ally. "What say you, Ms. Hughes? What is your response to Mr. Harrington's motion?"

"As I indicated in my response to Mr. Harrington's motion, I have spoken with Emma Jackson, and she has indicated to me that she was not willing to release her dental records nor is she willing to give fingerprints. She says it's an invasion of her privacy and frankly I agree. Emma Jackson is not a party to this case. She is a grieving sister. Now, I understand that the person in Mr. Porter's home at the time was not Ava Porter, at least the medical examiner, upon closer inspection, has indicated that the dental records do not match that of Ava Porter, but I submit that perhaps the Medical Examiner is incorrect about this. I have a copy of Mrs. Porter's dental records, and a copy of the dental records of the victim in this case, and I've had an expert examine both of these records. This expert can see very little difference between the two of them. He said there is a slight difference in one of the teeth, but the dental records of Ava Porter are quite old. She apparently has not seen a dentist in the past 10 years. Therefore, my expert cannot definitively say the dental records of the victim in this case do not match that of Mrs. Porter. There are differences between the dental records, but they're so slight that they could be caused by the fact that one dental record is 10 years old, the one obtained from Mrs. Porter's dentist, and one was taken just now, the dental records of the victim. There is bound to be changes anyway and my expert agrees with this."

"With all due respect, your honor, while Ms. Hughes is correct in that the changes between the two dental records are slight, I think it is incumbent on this court to make sure the person who died in that house was, in fact, Ava Porter. As you can see, Ava has an identical twin, so it's entirely possible the person who died in that house was Emma Jackson, not Ava Porter."

Judge Pruitt stared at me with a questioning look in his eyes. "Mr. Harrington, did your client, Mr. Porter, identify the person who died in the house as his wife?"

"Yes he did. I mean, he would have no reason to think otherwise. He was not even aware his wife had an identical twin. So, of course, he identified her as Ava Porter. But that didn't mean the person who died in the house was not actually her identical twin. And, frankly, I find it suspicious that the person known as Emma Jackson would be opposing this motion. If she had nothing to hide, she should freely want to give her dental records and her fingerprints."

Judge Pruitt looked over at Ally. "Ms. Hughes, why is Ms. Jackson refusing to give her fingerprints? That would be definitive as to whether or not the person who died in the house was Ava Porter or her identical twin. The dental records would also be helpful. However, because they were identical twins and apparently Ms. Ava Porter did not see a dentist on a regular basis, they might not be sufficient to identify the body with 100% accuracy. But the fingerprints would. Why would you not want to supply Ms. Jackson's fingerprints to the court?"

"With all due respect, Ms. Jackson believes that giving her fingerprints is an invasion of her privacy. And I agree with this. She feels that having her fingerprints on file would be akin to a Big Brother action. She simply does not want to give her fingerprints and I submit to the court that she should not be forced to. She is not a party to this court, she is not a party to this criminal action, so she is irrelevant to the case."

Judge Pruitt looked at both my motion and the response to it. Then he tapped his fingers lightly against one another. "With all due respect, Mr. Harrington, I find your argument hard to believe. You're telling me your client had no clue his wife had an identical twin? You're telling me your client would be intimate with someone and not realize the person he was with wasn't his wife but somebody else? The fact of the matter is, he identified her to the Medical Examiner. He told the Medical Examiner that the person who died was, in fact, his wife. He made a definitive identification, so the court will just have to go with that. If you can come up with any kind of evidence to the contrary, I'll be happy to hear it.

However, on this motion, I'm going to have to overrule it." He banged his gavel.

I wasn't ready to give up. "With all due respect, Your Honor, how am I supposed to get any kind of evidence about my theory unless you allow Emma Jackson to give her fingerprints? You're putting me into a Catch-22, where you're not allowing Emma Jackson to give her fingerprints because I don't have evidence that Ms. Jackson is actually Mrs. Porter. But I can't get that evidence unless you allow this motion."

"I'm sorry. But Ms. Jackson's right to privacy trumps your rather flimsy theory," Judge Pruitt said. "Ms. Hughes is actually correct. Ms. Jackson is not a party to this case, and, as such, she has a right to privacy that cannot be violated."

I sighed. I knew the real reason why the judge didn't order it. He was afraid. He was afraid that if he forced Emma, who I thought was really Ava, to give her fingerprints, she would file a lawsuit against him for invasion of privacy. The judge probably didn't want to deal with that.

So I was back at square one. I would have to find a way to prove to the jury what my theory was.

The only problem was, I still wasn't quite sure what my theory was. Even if the person who died in the house wasn't Ava, but Emma, so what? What did that prove? Plus, she was poisoned.

I was back to square one and I was back to pushing a boulder up a hill.

## Chapter Twenty-One

October 29 - The First Day of Trial

IT WAS the first day of trial, and I felt like I was as prepared as I could possibly be. After doing more investigation into this case, it suddenly came into view exactly what happened. At least, I think I knew what happened. It was a matter of proving it, however. That was always the rub. You could have an excellent theory to present, but if you couldn't prove it to a jury, you have nothing. In this case, my theory would be a crapshoot. To say the very least.

Harper agreed to second-chair me. I knew she would. I was happy she would be in the courtroom with me because I needed her help.

Harper was unsure about my strategy. She thought it was kind of crazy, to say the very least. She, too, found it hard to believe that Silas would have no clue his own wife had an identical twin. I didn't know why that was so hard for people to believe but it was. But once I got into the case, everything became clear as to why Ava and Emma did not get along, and why Ava never bothered to tell her husband about her twin sister.

It also became clear to me exactly why Emma, not Ava, died.

Unfortunately, I had one hurdle to clear – Ally had filed a motion *in limine* because she wanted to keep any kind of evidence out that the person who died in the house was not Ava Porter.

I saw Ally in the courtroom. "Why you gotta do me like this?" I said to Ally, only half teasing. "I think you know my very case hinges on whether or not I can bring in evidence about Emma and Ava, and in this case, the evidence is simply trying to cross-examine your witnesses." Ally had brought in both of Ava's parents, David, and Emma as witnesses. She would use them to establish that my client and Ava had a very strained relationship. My plan was to cross-examine them and try to break them down on the stand, but I would have to question them specifically on whether or not it was truly Ava who died in the house. When I thought about it, if I asked the right questions, I could probably establish what I needed to prove my theory.

"Of course I know your entire case hinges on whether or not you can question these witnesses on your theory. Why do you think I'm trying to prevent you from doing so? Listen, I hate to break this to you, but your client is a psycho. You know it, I know it. He's a dangerous man and he probably needs to be behind bars."

"That's a crappy thing to say. You're trying to prevent me from proving my case because you feel my client is psychotic and dangerous, and I dispute that, but even if he was, if he is not guilty of murdering his wife, then he doesn't belong behind bars… End of story."

"We'll see what the judge says today."

At that, we looked up and saw Judge Pruitt coming on the bench. "Remain seated," he said. "Now, as I understand it, this case is going to trial. And I also understand the prosecutor has a motion *in limine* she has filed. So, Mr. Harrington, Miss Hughes, please approach the bench and you can both give me your arguments. After I decide on this motion *in limine*, we will impanel a jury and get the show on the road. I also understand you, Mr. Harrington, also have a motion *in limine*. I'll hear yours first."

I cleared my throat. "My motion *in limine* is that the prosecutor cannot bring in the fact that my client, at the age of five, was involved in a fire where his mother was killed. The reason for my motion is very simple. There is some kind of evidence my client might have set the fire. Nothing has ever been proven, so I don't want this fire to even be brought up in front of the jury. I don't want the jury to infer my client was in any way, shape or form involved in it, and the only way to do so is to make sure the incident does not even come into evidence at all."

"That's a pretty open and shut motion," Judge Pruitt said. "Obviously, if there was no evidence your client was involved in setting the fire, and it happened when he was five years old, so even if he did set the fire, there's no way that fact can be brought in, there is no reason to even bring the fire into evidence. It's irrelevant."

I knew this motion *in limine* would be sustained. I had another one, however. I had a motion *in limine* to keep my client's mental health issues out of evidence. I knew Ally was aware my client had been in a mental hospital. She also was aware he had been diagnosed with narcissistic personality disorder. That was one thing I did not want brought into court. This would be a bit trickier, however. I had produced documents for Ally, at her request, about my client's stay in the hospital and about his diagnosis.

"My next motion *in limine* is for the fact my client has been in a mental hospital. He has been diagnosed with narcissistic personality disorder. I want to make sure this diagnosis does not come in."

It was surprisingly difficult to find case law on this matter. However, I also knew the physician-patient privilege was very hard to break. I knew the judge would side with me. My client's right to privacy was strong. At the same time, I knew the fact he'd been diagnosed with narcissistic personality disorder was something very relevant to the case. It was relevant to what Ally was trying to show – that my client was a cold-blooded killer. One who would not think twice about killing his wife just because he found out she was about to leave him for another man.

Just as I thought, however, Judge Pruitt nodded. "Motion sustained. Now, Ms. Hughes, do you have any motions for me?"

Ally nodded. "I filed a motion *in limine* to suppress any evidence that the defense might have that the person killed in the house was not Ava Porter. As you can remember, we were in court on this very issue several months ago, and you agreed with me that Mr. Harrington's theory was unlikely, and you also agreed that when he tried to prove it, it would be an invasion of privacy for Mrs. Porter's identical twin sister, Ms. Jackson. Ms. Emma Jackson is currently on the witness list and is scheduled to testify."

Judge Pruitt shook his head. "Your motion *in limine* is overruled. Mr. Harrington has the right to question witnesses. He has a right to cross-examine them, and if on cross-examination, he cares to question them about his theory, I will allow it." He looked at me. "Of course, that assumes Ms. Hughes opens the door on direct examination for such questions. I'm assuming she won't. I do see that all of Ms. Hughes' witnesses are also on your witness list. So I assume you'll have to ask these questions in your case in chief. Unless Ms. Hughes wants to cooperate and open the door on direct so you can cross-examine them." He looked over at Ally. "Now I don't want to tell you how to do your job, and I certainly don't want to dictate your strategy, but it might be worthwhile, and in the interest of expediency, for you to open that door on direct examination. You know Mr. Harrington will call all of your witnesses and he'll ask those questions in his direct examination. You might as well just kill two birds with one stone and open the door when you direct examine these witnesses. Just a suggestion to move things along."

I looked over at Ally. I didn't know if she would cooperate in that way, but she might. After all, the judge was right – if I couldn't cross-examine her witnesses on the matter, I would call them as my own witnesses. My entire case was dependent upon whether or not I could prove what I needed to prove on this matter and there was no way I would let that go.

She sighed. "I'll think about it."

She was defeated. I knew she was. At least, on this matter she was. "Listen, I know you don't want to cooperate with me, because I'm the defense attorney and you're the prosecutor. But the judge makes a good point. Either you open the door or I will. If you want to get done with this trial early, my suggestion is you open the door and allow me to cross-examine them on this issue."

She bristled. I saw her grit her teeth and hunch her shoulders. I knew she didn't want to give any kind of quarter to me. "I'll think about it."

Judge Pruitt looked at Ally. "Think hard about it. In the meantime, if there is no other motion *in limines* I need to entertain, I suggest we start bringing in the jury and starting our *voir dire*."

Within a half-hour, 50 men and women of all ages and colors were seated. 12 of them were seated in the jury box while the rest were seated in the gallery.

Ally started with her *voir dire*. She asked questions of the jurors about if they knew anybody involved in the case, and if they knew either the judge or the defense attorney or herself. She asked all the standard questions that people ask of jurors. With the raise of the hands, one by one people gave an answer.

And then it came to me. What I was looking for was somebody with an open mind. "Do you believe there are some people in this world who would willingly give their life to protect a person they loved?" This was a relevant question for me, because of the theory I was working on. The theory that had formulated over these past few months was that Emma Jackson was actually a willing participant in this entire scheme.

Several jurors raised their hands. I called on them one by one. They each said they thought there were people in the world who were that selfless. But all of them indicated they thought that kind of person was a rarity. To say the very least.

"What if a person was dying? Do you think it's out of the realm of possibility that a dying person, somebody who has only a few months to live as it is, would willingly give their lives to protect someone they loved?"

With that, more people raised their hands. "I believe that situation is very plausible," one man said. "After all, if you're already not long for this world, you might as well make your death count. Right?" He looked around at the other jurors, and he saw some of them were nodding their heads along. I made a note of the people nodding.

Another lady stood up. "I agree with this gentleman. I mean, if you have a terminal diagnosis, and you have a chance to help somebody close to you, why wouldn't you do it? Even if that brings your death on prematurely, at least you could die knowing you helped somebody."

I made a note of the people who agreed with this theory and would try to get each and every one of them on the jury. Unfortunately, I knew Ally was also making a note of the people who agreed with the statements and would try to keep them off the jury. But as long as I got at least a few of them, people who could possibly convince the other jurors my theory was correct, I'd have a chance with this case.

I asked a few more questions and then the potential jurors were asked to sit quietly while Ally and I made our selections. I started with some peremptory strikes and so did Ally. I had a couple of strikes for cause, and so did she. But after about 1/2 hour, we agreed on the 12 people who would be sitting on the jury and deciding Silas' fate. I got three of the people I wanted – three of the people who I knew agreed with the statement that if somebody is dying, it is a good thing to use your death to help somebody else out. I knew that with those jurors on the panel, my argument would be at least halfway there.

The jury was picked, so we all took a break, and when we came back, it would be time to begin.

I knew I had a battle in front of me, but I thought it was a battle I could win.

## Chapter Twenty-Two

ALLY WAS the first to give her statement. "Ladies and gentlemen of the jury," she began. "You're going to hear a story that will be hard to hear. To say the very least. It's a story of a man, Mr. Silas Porter, who is a very troubled man. You will hear evidence on just how troubled his relationship was with Ms. Ava Porter. The evidence will show that Ms. Ava Porter displayed bruises when she visited her parents. Her parents will testify that they strongly suspected Mrs. Porter was being physically abused by the defendant, Silas Porter. The evidence will also show Mr. and Mrs. Porter had a volatile relationship, to say the very least. Mrs. Porter had sought and obtained two restraining orders against him because she was fearful for her life. She was fearful about what he would do to her."

"You will hear the evidence propounded by an expert witness, an expert on the field of domestic abuse. This expert will testify that a woman is most in danger when she is threatening to leave her abuser. You will also hear evidence that this is exactly what had happened here. You will hear evidence from both of Mrs. Porter's parents and her fiancé, David Taylor. Mr. Taylor is a golf pro and a friend of the family, and he and Mrs. Porter had begun a relationship while Mr. Porter was in Europe on a business trip. By the time Mr. Porter got back from his business trip, the victim, Ava Porter, was already engaged to Mr. Taylor and had already told Mr. Porter she would be leaving him in favor of Mr. Taylor."

"Here is what happened in this case, ladies and gentlemen. First, the defendant chained the victim to a wall in a guesthouse he had behind his main house. This was a guesthouse used for people who were staying overnight. It was not, contrary to what Mr. Porter will try to tell you, a dungeon for BDSM activities. It was nothing more than a simple guesthouse. He chained her to this wall and made her helpless. Then he set the guest house on fire."

Ally approached the jurors, and looked at them one by one in the eye. "Imagine that. Imagine being made helpless by your husband. Imagine your husband is 6'3" and 190 pounds and in amazing shape, while you are only 5'5" and 110 pounds. Imagine him carrying you to a building, and then forcefully putting your hands into a pair of handcuffs attached to a wall. Try to imagine her terror as she realized what he was doing. Accelerant was found at the scene. He deliberately set that fire and he murdered his wife in this gruesome manner."

"This is a very disturbed mind, the mind of this defendant. Only a disturbed mind would do something like that. Only someone depraved would make sure his wife died in such agony. And that's exactly what Mr. Porter is. He is depraved."

She paced back and forth. "Think about it ladies and gentlemen. Think about what kind of person would make sure he not just murdered his wife but murdered her in such a way that she died in agony." She pointed at Silas. "And that's exactly what this man did. This man who is before you – he is an animal. No, scratch that. To call him an animal is an insult to animals everywhere. This man is someone who is deeply, deeply disturbed. And he deserves to be behind bars for the rest of his life. Only there, in a prison, will society be safe from him. That is why I urge you to find the defendant guilty of murdering his wife. I urge you to find him guilty and I urge you to sentence him to the maximum sentence possible. He deserves to spend the rest of his life behind bars."

"Thank you very much."

Ally sat down and I stood up. I cleared my throat. "Ladies and gentlemen of the jury, you heard the prosecutor's arguments. And they sound compelling. I would agree with you. I'm not going to argue that there were restraining orders against my client. It would be pointless to argue that point, because there were restraining orders against him. However, that is the only fact I will stipulate to, because everything else the prosecutor told you has been a lie."

"Are you going to hear evidence that Ava's parents noticed she had bruises on her arms? Yes, you are going to hear evidence about that. However, you will also hear evidence from my client about where those bruises came from. He will testify the bruises came not from him but from other men who she was seeing. You see, Ava was a submissive. I'm not sure what the jury knows about the concept of BDSM – bondage – discipline – sadism – masochism. What I can tell you is that my client, Mr. Porter, and the victim, Ava Porter, were involved in a dominant-submissive relationship. Mr. Porter will testify as to what kind of relationship they had and how it involved bondage. And my client will testify that this was as far as they went. He would bind Mrs. Porter during sex – he would put her in a body bag, or into a small box, and restrict breathing. He would use handcuffs with her. Blindfolds. And other elements like that. However, they were not involved in the more physical aspects of the BDSM relationship. Specifically, my client will testify he did not want to beat his wife. Or whip her. However, she desired that, so he allowed her to take other sexual partners. People who would do that for her. He knew she needed that and allowed her to stray."

"So that's where those bruises came from. Not from my client, but from the other men my client's wife, Ava Porter, was seeing on the side. She was seeing these men with the express consent of my client, Silas Porter. He, too, had other sexual partners. That was the nature of their relationship – it was open. They allowed one another to see other people."

"So, that is one piece of evidence that will refute what the prosecutor says. You will hear my client testify to the fact they had an open relationship, therefore, if Mrs. Porter would be seeing another man while he was in Europe, he would not be angry enough to kill her."

"Now what about the restraining orders? Well, those restraining orders were levied against my client five years ago, at a time my client was going through a very dark period. He sought help for it. He will admit he threatened Ava's safety two times during their marriage. Their fights got physical twice. Again, this was five years ago, and he has sought help for his issues since then. There have been no incidents since."

I knew the restraining orders would be a problem for me. However, the fact that they were so long ago worked in our favor. I hoped the jury bought the story that my client was a changed man. I knew he really wasn't – once you are diagnosed with a personality disorder, such as narcissistic personality disorder, it's very tough to overcome that. Personality disorders were not amenable to drugs or even to therapy. They were pretty much intractable. But since I knew the jury wouldn't be allowed to hear evidence about his personality disorder, the prosecution would be at a disadvantage in proving my client and Ava had an abusive relationship.

I continued on. "You will also hear evidence that the person who died in that dungeon was not Ava Porter at all, but was, rather, her identical twin sister, Emma Jackson." I would be walking on dangerous ground. I was hoping I could prove what I needed to prove, but I wasn't sure at all. Therefore I figured it was best to leave the opening statement at that.

The only way I could prove my theory was by breaking down the parents, David, and the person posing as Emma Jackson – actually Ava Porter. However, I was not at all sure my questioning would have the desired effect.

I looked at the jury's faces and they were looking very skeptical, and decided to go on after all. "Yes, the victim in this case, Ava Porter, had an identical twin. Her name was Emma Jackson. You'll hear evidence that Emma Jackson took Ava Porter's place and she was the one who died. You will also hear evidence that the person who died in that dungeon was not killed by the fire. Granted, the fire that swept through the dungeon was swift and hot because it was set by an accelerant. However, Emma Jackson, the person who actually died in that house, was dead before the fire swept in. She was dead because she was poisoned. You will hear evidence from the medical examiner that traces of the barbiturate Secobarbital were found in the tissues of Emma Jackson."

"When I present my evidence, you as a jury will have no choice but to find my client not guilty of the murder of his wife, Ava Porter. Thank you very much for your time and attention, and I ask you in advance to find my client not guilty of murder."

I sat down and glanced at the jury. They were curious, that was for sure. I got their attention.

Could I prove any of this?

That was the question of the day.

## Chapter Twenty-Three

AFTER WE DID our opening statements, the jury took a short break. I sat down and looked over at Harper. "What do you think? Do you think I convinced the jury?"

Harper smiled and shook her head. "You have your work cut out for you, I'll tell you that. I mean, you'll have to convince a jury the victim in this case isn't really dead, but will be taking the stand, posing as her identical twin. If anybody can convince a jury of something like that, it would be you. But I wish you luck."

I sighed. I was excited, however, for the Medical Examiner to testify. I knew Ally had her independent expert who had looked over the dental records. The Medical Examiner herself was not entirely certain the dental records were not a match. She, too, made the point that Ava had not seen a dentist in 10 years. Therefore the slight changes between the dental records taken from the corpse and the dental records shown by Ava's last visit to the dentist could be easily explained away.

It was just my luck Ava Porter was not somebody who

kept up with yearly dental appointments. Granted, a lot of people were like that. Nobody likes dentists. I, myself, was way overdue for my own dental appointment. But I had been to the dentist within the past five years. It surprised me that Ava wouldn't have gone to see a dentist on a regular basis. She was so focused on her physical appearance and her body that I imagined she would be more diligent about the dentist thing, but she apparently wasn't.

The irony was, apparently Emma *was* the kind of person who saw dentists on a regular basis. I managed to get her dental records from Anna. Of course, since Anna obtained them illegally, there was no way I could possibly use them in court. Emma's dental records matched the dental records of the corpse almost perfectly. Unfortunately, there was no way I could get these records into evidence.

In fact, the Medical Examiner would be the second witness Ally would call. Her first witness was the officer on the scene. While I really had a lot of questions for him, I was most interested in what the Medical Examiner had to say, mainly because she would testify about the poison. Ally never mentioned the fact that a poison was found in the victim's system.

However, there were also a few questions I wanted to ask the officer on the scene who cordoned off the dungeon. I wanted to make sure the jury knew the state of the house was such that you couldn't really tell what it was. Therefore, it was possible that the house was, in fact, a dungeon and not a guesthouse. That was important to me, because I had to show the jury that the kind of relationship Ava had with Silas was such that there was consensual sex play. That was the only way I could explain how Ava had bruises on her arms. My client would testify to this fact as well, but it would be more helpful if I could show that Ava and Silas actually had a dungeon on their property.

The officer on the scene, Officer King, was sworn in, and Ally asked him a series of questions about how he came to the scene. "I was called to the scene because the next-door neighbor of Mr. and Mrs. Porter contacted the fire department when she saw the flames in the back of the Porters' house. I was the first responder, along with the fire marshal, Craig Sutton, and his crew."

"And what did you find when you went to the scene?" Ally asked.

"I found a structure that had been burned completely to the ground. There was one thing left of the structure, and that was a brick wall, with two handcuffs attached to it. In those handcuffs were the remains of a woman, the deceased, who I identified as a female probably between the ages of 25 and 35. She had been very badly burned, to the extent that there was very little left of her, except for the hands still in those handcuffs, some bones, and very little tissue. Most of it was burned."

At this, Ally presented to the jury her blown-up pictures of the charred remains of the victim. "Can you please identify these pictures?"

He nodded. "These are the pictures I took of the crime scene." He pointed at the victim whose hands were still in the handcuffs. "This is an accurate representation of the body I found in that structure. It was a body later identified by Mr. Porter as being that of his wife."

I sighed as Ally dramatically took the blown-up pictures over to the jury and showed them what "Ava" looked like at that time. One thing was certain – these pictures were extremely gruesome. The way Ally told it, Ava died in the worst way possible. I saw members of the jury visibly shutter, as Ally stood there for several minutes showing them the pictures of the charred victim.

"Did you question Mr. Porter at the scene?"

"Yes I did."

"And what did he tell you about what happened that night?"

"He explained that he and his wife, Mrs. Porter, were engaged in sex games in what he called his dungeon. Apparently, he called the structure in the back of the house his dungeon. He said he had chained his wife to the wall because she enjoyed that kind of bondage. He said he was being intimate with his wife when she suddenly gasped for air and said she couldn't breathe and then she died. Right after she died, the fire swept through that structure, a wildfire he said he barely escaped himself. That was what he told me."

Ally nodded. "I have nothing further for this witness."

She sat down and I approached the officer. "Officer King, you stated on direct examination that the only thing left of the structure behind the pool was a brick wall and a pair of handcuffs attached to the wall. Is that right?"

"Yes, that's correct."

"So, is it fair to say that the structure could very well have been a dungeon and not a guesthouse?"

"Yes. It would be fair to say that. There was very little left of the structure by the time I got there. Everything had burned."

I showed him a picture I had taken of the crime scene. It was a picture of the structure that had burned to the ground. It was nothing but a burned pile of rubble and the wall that was sturdy enough to stand. "I'm going to show you a picture of a structure behind the Porter's house. Is this a fair and accurate representation of the structure you came upon when you were called to the scene?"

He took a careful look at the picture. He handed it back to me. "Yes. That is a very accurate representation of the structure I came upon when I was called to the scene."

"And do you see in this picture that nothing was left of the structure except for this brick wall?"

"Yes. That's what I indicated on the direct examination as well. Apparently the fire had burned hot enough to burn everything to the ground."

"So is it fair to say it's impossible to tell what the structure had been before it burned?"

"Yes. That is correct."

"Now, you stated on direct that my client had said his wife was dead before the fire swept in, and that the reason why she was attached to the wall was because they were participating in sex games and his wife enjoyed being bound. Is that right?"

"Yes. That's what he said."

"I have nothing further for this witness."

"Ms. Hughes," Judge Pruitt said to Ally. "Please call your next witness."

"The state calls Dr. Prorock."

Dr. Prorock, the medical examiner, approached the bench. She was the person who I really wanted to question, the person who I was excited about questioning. Well, him and Ava's parents, David, and the person posing as Emma, but I knew was really Ava. I was looking forward to questioning all of these people, but I had to start with the Medical Examiner, who would cast doubt on the dental records matching between Ava and the deceased victim. While I knew Ally could rehabilitate Dr. Prorock after I cross-examined her, I also knew she, if I did things right, would put doubt into the jury's mind as to who was in that dungeon when the fire swept in.

Dr. Prorock was sworn in and Ally got right to work. "Dr. Prorock, you were the medical examiner in this case, is that correct?"

"Yes. I was."

"And did you have occasion to examine the remains of the victim in this case, Ava Porter?"

"Yes I did."

"And what was the condition of the body when you examined it?"

"The body was extremely burned. The fire that swept through the structure where she was trapped was apparently so hot that there was very little left of the victim by the time I examined her. The lungs and most of her vital organs were little more than ash. In fact, the only intact part of her was her hands. They were attached to the wall, and apparently that was why they were intact and the rest of her was not."

"Were you able to determine the cause of death, then?"

"No. I was not."

"And why were you not able to ascertain the cause of death?"

"Because of the condition of the lungs, which were so severely burned I could not examine them, as they were the consistency of ash by the time the victim was brought to me, I could not ascertain if the deceased was alive at the time the fire had swept into the structure. Ordinarily, the condition of the lungs would be what I would examine in ascertaining if the person was alive at the time of a fire. The lungs and the throat. Typically, in a burning death, if the person was alive when he or she encountered the fire, I could see if the person had inhaled smoke. The throat would be severely burned and the lungs would show a great deal of smoke inhalation. Unfortunately, that was impossible to ascertain in this case. Because the victim was so badly burned, I could not do my usual examination on her."

Ally nodded. It wasn't what she wanted to hear – I knew that. The Medical Examiner could no more do an autopsy on "Ava's" remains then she could do an autopsy on somebody who had been cremated. That was how badly burned body "Ava" was. I knew that was by design – according to my theory, Ava never wanted anybody to know who really was killed in that house. She wanted the body to be so badly burned that she could not be identified. Unfortunately for her, there were a few things that survived on the body. The teeth, the hands, and enough tissue that the Medical Examiner could tell there was poison found in her system.

"I have nothing further for this witness."

Ally sat down and I stood up. "Now, Dr. Prorock, you testified on direct that it was impossible to tell if the victim was alive at the time the fire swept in. Is that correct?"

"Yes, that is correct."

"However, is it true you found traces of a powerful barbiturate called Secobarbital in some of the tissues you were able to test?"

"Yes, that is true. While most of the vital organs and lungs in the throat were charred beyond recognition, I was able to test some of the tissues in the hands. In those tissues I discovered trace amounts of a barbiturate called Secobarbital."

"So it's possible the deceased had expired before the fire swept in and perhaps died of the poisoning?"

"Yes. That is possible."

"What do you know about the barbiturate called Secobarbital?"

"It's a barbiturate, which means it slows the heart rate down. It also slows breathing and lowers the blood pressure and tends to relax the muscles."

"But you couldn't tell how much the deceased had taken of this drug before she died, isn't that correct?"

"Yes. I wasn't able to examine her liver, which is where the drug is processed. I was only able to test a very limited amount of tissue from the deceased's fingertips, so I could not determine if the deceased took a fatal amount."

"But if the deceased was in the end stages of pancreatic cancer, is it fair to say the Secobarbital could be fatal in a small dose?"

"Yes, that is fair to say."

"And you were able to also obtain a dental record from the deceased, isn't that true?"

"Yes. Her bones were, by and large, intact. And that would include her teeth."

"Now, I provided you with a copy of Ava Porter's dental records, is that correct?"

"Yes, you provided those to me."

"And did the dental impression of the deceased match the dental records I provided you of Ava Porter?"

"Actually, there were some differences between the two. For instance, the teeth of the deceased had a slightly different wear pattern than the dental records I examined. However, the differences were extremely slight."

"But you're telling the jury the dental records obtained for the deceased were different from the records I provided for you that were identified as that of Ava Porter. Isn't that right?"

"Yes. That is right."

"I have nothing further to this witness."

At that, Ally approached the witness. She would have to redirect her. She cleared her throat. "Dr. Prorock, you stated on direct that the dental impressions of the deceased did not match the dental records provided, which were the dental records of Ava Porter. Isn't that right?"

"Yes. That is correct."

"However, the dental records you were provided for Mrs. Porter were 10 years old. Is that not also correct?"

"Yes. That is correct."

"It would be in fact unusual if these dental impressions would closely match dental records taken so long ago, wouldn't it?"

"Yes. Everybody's teeth moves over the year and teeth also wear down over time. Gums recede. So yes, it would be highly unusual to match up dental records taken from 10 years ago and match them up perfectly to dental impressions taken today. That said, the differences were slight."

"Can you say with 100% authority that the dental records you examined from the deceased were not those of Ava Porter?"

She shook her head. "No. I cannot say that with 100% certainty."

"I have nothing further."

I had to concede that it looked bad that Dr. Prorock was unable to establish with certainty that the person in that dungeon was not Ava Porter. However, I hoped the medical examiner at least put a doubt in the jury's mind that it wasn't her. She couldn't say the dental records didn't match, but she also couldn't say they did. That left it open.

I was still in the game. That was all that mattered.

The next person who Ally decided to call was her expert

on spousal abuse. I had deposed her and knew what she would say. I also knew how to cross-examine her.

The expert that Ally called was a psychologist by the name of Dr. Owen. Dr. Owen was a therapist with 30 years experience in the field of domestic violence. She had a practice that specialized in treating women suffering from domestic violence and also specialized in treating the PTSD that resulted from these incidents. She was a circuit lecturer on the topic of domestic violence and was an expert witness on behalf of women. One of her specialties was testifying in cases where women used the battered spouse syndrome defense – this was a defense that was sometimes used when a woman had been battered and would end up murdering her husband. Dr. Owen was somebody who had testified in hundreds of trials and had treated thousands of clients. She was Harvard educated and there was very little I could do to impugn her credentials. So I wasn't even going to try that. I would simply make the point that she had not treated my client nor had she treated Ava.

Dr. Own was sworn in, and Ally approached her. "Dr. Owen, you are here to testify today in this case. Can you please tell the jury a little bit about your credentials? Explain why you are an expert on this issue?"

She got closer to the microphone. "Yes. I am a psychologist, and I specialize in treating women who have been victims of domestic violence. In fact, I have treated thousands of women over the past 30 years. I've treated them for post-traumatic stress disorder as well – this is a disorder that often occurs when women have been badly abused and they relive the incidents again and again. That has been my specialty, and I have testified in 300 expert trials on behalf of women who have been involved in domestic violence.

I've also given lectures around the country on this issue. I received my PhD in psychology from Harvard University."

"And you have been pursuing your specialty for the past 30 years, is that correct?"

"Yes. That is correct."

"Do you treat other kinds of patients as well? Patients who have not been involved in domestic violence situations?"

"No. I concentrate only on women involved in abusive situations."

Ally paced back and forth in front of her. "And I want to make it clear to the jury that you did not actually treat Ava Porter, is that correct?"

"Yes, that is correct."

"Now, in your professional opinion, in your expert opinion, when is a volatile situation, an abusive situation, most likely to result in the death of the abused partner?"

"The most dangerous time in a volatile situation, where one partner is being severely abused by another, is when that partner has made plans to leave the abusive partner. That's because the abuser has a need for power and control over the abused. And when the abuser is certain he's going to lose that power and control over his abused spouse, he often becomes homicidal. If the situation is going to become homicidal, it is often when the abused partner makes plans to leave."

"I have nothing further for this witness."

I stood up and approached Dr. Owen. "Now, Dr. Owen, you stated on direct you did not actually treat Ava Porter. I just wanted to make that clear to the jury."

"Yes. That is correct. I did not treat Ava Porter."

"So you don't actually know if Ava Porter was being abused by my client, Silas Porter, do you?"

"No, I do not know if that is the case. That is not why I'm testifying. I'm simply testifying about the point that the state wanted to make, which is that the most dangerous time in a volatile domestic violence situation is when the abused makes plans to leave. That is the only thing I'm testifying to. I do not know if the woman involved in this case was actually abused."

"I have nothing further for this witness."

So far, I felt I was trying to stay a little bit ahead of the witnesses, but none of the witnesses were quite clear. The officer wasn't clear about the state of the structure that burned down – he couldn't tell if it was a dungeon or a simple guesthouse. The medical examiner wasn't clear as to whether or not the dental records match that of Ava. And this witness wasn't clear that Ava was not being abused. I thought that each witness was a bit of a wash, but, at the same time, if I were to gauge the strength of the case at this point, I would have to admit the prosecution was probably slightly ahead.

I hoped I could change that though.

By this time, it was 5 o'clock, and it was time for everyone to go home. "Ladies and gentlemen of the jury, we shall recess until tomorrow morning at 9 AM," Judge Pruitt announced after Dr. Owen left the stand. "Tomorrow, I expect everybody to be in their seats right at 9 AM because we're going to start at that time. Thank you very much for your service today, and I shall see all of you back here tomorrow at 9 AM."

## Chapter Twenty-Four

I GOT HOME from my first day of trial, and I was treated to a very unpleasant surprise. Gretchen came up to me, and looked like she was about ready to shake me. "I've been trying to get a hold of you," she said. "And so has the school."

I sighed. This did not sound good. To say the least. "What's going on?"

"Nate's been taken into custody," she said. "He brought a gun to the school this morning."

My reaction to finding out my 10-year-old son brought a gun to his school was probably more muted than it should've been. Part of me was shocked and horrified, but another part of me was not really all that surprised. Nate was troubled. Worse, he still wasn't talking to me and I had no idea where he got that gun. I had a gun but I had it locked up. I always felt I needed protection because of my background and history. I was always looking over my shoulder because I had to. It was a force of habit, after I got out of the joint, to make sure I always had a piece at home. I just never dreamed Nate would get a hold of it.

"Guess I better go down to the detention center and find out what's going on."

Nate's school was going to install metal detectors and make all the kids bring in clear backpacks, but somehow those steps were not taken. Too many parents protested and the school administrators backed down. I had gone to the meetings, to voice my opinion, which was I thought the metal detectors and the clear backpack ideas were sound, but I was overruled.

And now my son was apparently in detention for bringing in a gun. I knew he was troubled, but with my being so busy with the trial, I just couldn't give him the time and attention I needed to give him. I felt horribly guilty about that as I got into my car, after telling Gretchen I would appreciate it if she stayed with Amelia while I took care of this matter.

It was just what I didn't need in the middle of a trial, but that was how life worked sometimes. Sometimes your kid ends up being nabbed for having a gun at school in the middle of a trial and you just had to deal with it.

The juvenile detention center was a part of the family justice complex on 26th and Gillham. It was right across the street from the Crown Center and a large church, Our Lady of Sorrows, which was built in the 1920s by German immigrants. I sped down there, parked the car, and sprinted into the detention center. "Hi," I said to the armed receptionist. "My son, Nate Harrington, has been picked up and he's in detention right now." I showed her my bar card. "As you can see, I'm an attorney and I need to see my son right away."

She buzzed me back to the detention facility. I went into

a small room with poor lighting and a long table and waited to see my son. He came out in five minutes. He was still in his street clothes and was not in handcuffs but was accompanied by an armed guard. He hung his head when he saw me but didn't say a word.

"Nate, I'm going to speak with the juvenile officer after I speak with you, but I think I can probably take you home tonight." That was the way it worked in the 16th circuit. Normally juveniles who are picked up are returned to a custodial parent unless there are extenuating circumstances. If there were extenuating circumstances, then a juvenile may be kept for 24 hours if the juvenile officer deems it necessary, or they may be held for longer, but they must have a hearing within 24 to 48 hours if they're going to be detained. "But do you mind telling me why you took my gun to school?"

He said nothing but just shook his head. I gathered I would have to speak with the officer in charge to find out why Nate would do that.

"Listen kid, I've been where you are," I said. "Pissed-off at the world. Thinking nobody was hearing me. I couldn't find anybody to listen to me. I certainly couldn't talk to my mother." I didn't say anything more about my mom to Nate. He didn't know the problems I had with my mom growing up. I never told him about her issues, because he was very close to my mom and I didn't want that to change. When he went to visit my mom, he came alive. He actually talked, because my mom had a way of getting him to communicate. She was a lot of things, most of them not good, but she related well to Nate, and that was important to me. I took a deep breath. "Anyhow, believe it or not, I know how you feel."

A part of me didn't want to tell him I knew how he felt.

I always hated it when people would say that to me. Of course they didn't know how I felt. How could they possibly know how I felt? Unless they were in my shoes, with an abusive stepfather and a drunk mother whoring herself, they couldn't possibly relate to what I was going through. It was sheer desperation that led me to shoot my stepfather while he slept. I truly thought he would kill either me or my mom, maybe both of us. It was the darkest time in my life, even darker than the time I spent in prison, because at that time I had nobody on my side. By the time I got to prison, I had the guys on my side, so things weren't nearly as bad at that time as they were when I killed my stepfather.

Nate, of course, was not dealing with anything near what I was at that time. But that didn't matter. Whatever was troubling him was real to him. His desperation was as palpable to him as mine was to me, and I had to realize that. I just wished I could get into his head and figure out what was really bothering him so much. I knew he missed Sarah desperately. After the Amelia debacle, Sarah disappeared altogether with her boyfriend. She was not going to resurface, not after what she did to me and Amelia. She tried to terminate my parental rights to Amelia and that was the end of it for me. At the same time, I asked her to maintain a relationship with Nate, just because of how he felt about her. She refused, so Nate had not heard from her for many months.

He just shrugged.

I went and found the juvenile officer, because I needed to talk to her about what Nate had done at school that day. What had set him off and made him take the gun to school. I hated that Nate himself did not feel he could speak with me about that, but it was what it was. He wouldn't talk to me, except for in his own time, so, in the meantime, I was simply going to have to talk to other people who knew what was going on.

The juvenile officer involved in the case was named Terry Warner. I met her in her office. "I decided not to ask for a 24-hour hold for Nate, so you're free to take him home tonight," Terry said. "Of course you know the drill, so you know there will be a hearing on his case in the near future. He's going to have to be arraigned and there will have to be a trial, just like in an adult case. In the meantime, it's my understanding that Nate will be suspended from school and maybe even expelled. That's not my concern, of course, but I wanted to give you a heads up about that."

I nodded. I had represented juveniles in the juvenile court before, so she was right – I knew the drill. I just hoped it would never come to this. I had hoped that neither one of my kids would ever be involved in the juvenile system, like I was when I was their age, but apparently these hopes were not to be. I would obviously have to speak with the school administrators about hopefully having Nate remain in school. The last thing I wanted was for him to be expelled from school, because that would make his life even more unstable than it was. I understood why the school wanted to expel him, of course, but I hoped they would change their mind about that.

"Can you tell me what happened? Do you have any idea why Nate would have brought a gun to school?"

"From what I understand, after speaking with some of the kids in school, Nate was being bullied by a boy by the name of James Royal. From what the kids told me, James has decided that Nate is gay, and he's been bullying him about that for months. He's gotten the other kids into the act, bullying and teasing him, and from what his best friend, Charles Whitford, told me, Nate had had enough. Nate himself refuses to talk to me, but he talked to Charles, who talked to me. Charles told me Nate told him that he would end the bullying once and for all. So he brought the gun into the school and started flashing it around in his classroom, and he even aimed it at James and threatened him with it. The teacher immediately called 911 and the officers arrived to take Nate into custody."

I thought about what Officer Warner was telling me. James was bullying Nate about being gay. I wondered if it was true. If it was, then that would explain a lot of things – why Nate had been so silent and sullen. Why he had clammed up and just decided to quit speaking with me about his feelings. I had assumed he was just troubled because of the divorce from Sarah, but maybe there was something more. Maybe Nate was struggling with himself.

Was Nate struggling with his identity? He was only 10 years old, but I knew a great many people who were gay knew it from a very young age. Not that this was Nate's problem – it could very well be this James person was just looking for an excuse to pick on him. At the same time, I needed to let him know that if he needed to speak with me about whether or not he was gay, he could. I knew he had this mistaken idea that I was some kind of macho man who wouldn't understand problems such as questioning sexuality. It didn't make me entirely comfortable to ask him about it, but I knew I would have to try.

"Thanks for talking with me," I said to Officer Warner. "I'm sure I'll see you in court for Nate's court date."

I went through the paperwork to have Nate released to me and I got Nate to take him home. We got in the car, and I looked at him.

"Nate, buddy, I told you earlier you can talk to me about

anything. And that means you can talk to me about anything. Absolutely anything. I hope you know that."

He looked at me and opened his mouth. It looked like he was about ready to say something.

But what came out of his mouth was something I was not prepared for.

"I took the gun to school because I wanted to threaten James. But it wasn't just him I wanted to threaten. It was also my teacher, Mrs. Bowen." He looked out the window. "She's touched me, dad. She's touched me in a bad place."

## Chapter Twenty-Five

NATE TOLD me about what happened with his teacher Mrs. Bowen, and I knew I would have to see her right at that moment. I also called Harper, because I needed her to possibly take the lead on the trial for the morning session. I had a feeling I would be talking with the police about Mrs. Bowen, or, at the very least, I would be dealing with the matter in one way or another.

I called Harper and she understood. "Of course," she said. "That's what second-chairs are for." And she was right about that. A second-chair for a trial was a bit like an understudy for a play - if something happens to the lead, the understudy is ready to take the reins. I knew Harper knew Silas's case as much as I did, so I felt confident she could step in and take control of the trial.

I had Mrs. Bowen's address and I drove right over to her house. She lived in a modest Tudor- style house in the Leawood area, which was by the school itself. I knew she was married to an attorney, but his specialty was personal injury, so I didn't really know him all that well.

I went right up to her door and knocked on it. She answered it within a few minutes. When I saw her, I knew she had been drinking quite a bit. I tried to tamp down my rage before opening my mouth. I couldn't lose control – that would not do anybody any good. "Mrs. Bowen, I'm Nate Harrington's father. I need to speak with you right now."

She looked around, as if she was afraid somebody would hear her talking to me. "I knew you would be coming to see me tonight, after what happened with Nate in school today. I'm very sorry about that – I knew James had been harassing Nate for months and I didn't do enough about it. I guess that in hindsight, what Nate ended up doing was foreseeable. I should have done more to make sure it didn't come to this."

"Are you alone?" I asked her. "Because I need to speak with you alone."

She nodded. "My husband is away on a business trip. So yes, I am alone. Would you like to come in?"

I looked over at Nate who was looking at me from inside the car. "With all due respect, my son is in the car, and he does not want to come out. So no, I don't want to come in. But I do need to speak with you."

She stepped out and closed the door behind her. "Okay," she said. "What do you need to speak with me about?"

I took a deep breath. "Nate told me about what you've been doing to him for the past few months. I called the cops, and they'll be here within a few –" At that, I heard the unmistakable sound of a siren, and I saw the cops pull up in front of her house.

"What the hell is going on?" she asked me. "Why did you call the cops on me?"

"I think you know. I'm going to the station and I'm going to tell them what Nate told me. I just wanted to give you a fair warning. I also wanted to tell you that if you ever come near my son again, he won't be the one with the gun, but I will be. And I won't have the gun because I needed somebody's attention. I'll have that gun because I'm going to use it." I didn't tell her I had experience with killing people with a gun, namely my stepfather when I was 15, but that thought was in my mind. All I could think about was that I was capable of anything to protect the people I loved. And that meant absolutely anything.

I saw the cops talk to Mrs. Warner, who started crying hysterically as they led her into the squad car. The cops drove off, and I followed them. I would give a statement and tell them what Nate had told me. That was the only way they would have probable cause to arrest her.

I got down to the station and talked to the officer in charge of this case. After about an hour of talking to this officer, I was informed that Mrs. Warner was, indeed, arrested for molesting my son. Apparently, she gave them a confession, and broke down crying.

This was only the beginning. I knew I had my work cut out for me with Nate. I would have to talk to his therapist about what was going on, as well as getting Nate himself to see the same therapist. I would have to press the case against Mrs. Warner in court. For now, I did my duty as far as talking to the cops about what was going on. This was the first step in what would be a very long process.

As I drove Nate home, I looked at him. "Thank you very much for finally telling me what's going on with you. I'm going to make an appointment with our family therapist as soon as I can." I didn't really know what else to say. I didn't want to make things worse, and I was afraid that anything I said at that point would do just that – make things worse.

"Whatever, Dad." He continued to look out the window.

"I know you don't want to talk to that therapist, but Nate, you need to." The therapist I had found for me, Nate, and Amelia was a good one. I had faith in her. Nate always had problems opening up to her, but I hoped tonight would be a turning point.

One thing was for sure – Nate needed help. He needed professional help, and he needed to make sure I was by his side the whole time.

I knew that in the coming weeks and months, I would find out more about what Mrs. Warner did to my son.

And I would probably want to kill her myself.

## Chapter Twenty-Six

THE NEXT DAY, I got into court. Harper was already there, working feverishly on her cross-examination of the Jacksons, who I knew would be first on the prosecutor's list for the morning. She looked up when she saw me, and came over and gave me a hug. "How are you doing?" She shook her head. "I couldn't stop thinking about you last night, or Nate. I couldn't imagine being in your shoes. If that happened to either one of my girls, I think I would probably have to kill that person."

I took a deep breath. "I'm just going to have to compartmentalize so I can win this case. After I win this case, I'm going to have to turn all my mental energy into making sure Nate does not become one of my clients one day."

"Do you still want me to take the lead on this case?"

"No. I think I'm okay. Last night, mentally, I was in a bad place. A very bad place. But this morning, I got my fighting spirit back, and I decided I to take the bull by the horns and win this case. So no, I'll be okay."

She put her arm around me. "Okay, but if you need to step away, I'll be happy to help. You know that."

"Thanks. I know I can count on you."

After about 20 minutes, the jury had come in, and the prosecutor was in place. The bailiff announced the arrival of the judge, we all rose when he came in and sat down again. "Okay, I'm going to once again call the case of the State of Missouri v. Parker. Ms. Hughes, call your first witness."

"The state calls Opal Jackson."

I looked around and saw Opal coming through the door and she approached the witness stand. The bailiffs swore her in and she sat down.

Ally approached her. "Please state your name for the record," she said.

Opal leaned closer into the microphone. "Opal Rosemary Jackson," she said.

"And Ms. Jackson, can you please tell the court what your relationship is to the accused and to the deceased?"

"Yes. I am the mother of Ava Porter, and the accused, Silas Porter, is my son-in-law. Or he was my son-in-law. Now, he has no relation to me."

"Now, to your knowledge, did your daughter have a healthy marriage with Mr. Porter?"

She shook her head. "No. They did not have a healthy relationship."

"What kind of relationship did they have?"

She sat up straighter in her chair. "They had a relationship that was abusive."

I stood up. " Objection Your Honor, the witness stated a conclusion. Move to strike."

"Motion to strike sustained," Judge Pruitt said. "Counselor, please rephrase your question. Your previous question called for a conclusion, so the witness can hardly be blamed for giving one."

Ally nodded. "What specific incidents would cause you to believe that Mr. and Mrs. Porter did not have a healthy relationship?"

"I saw bruises on my daughter's body. On her arms. She tried to hide them, because when she would come to visit, she would always wear long sleeves. But one day, I dropped in on her in her home. She was wearing short sleeves, and I saw bruises all over her arms. I asked her what happened and she didn't give me a good answer. I knew the truth. She didn't have to tell me. After all, there were restraining orders against Silas. I had a pretty good indication as to where those bruises came from."

"Now you mentioned that your daughter had restraining orders against Mr. Porter. During this period of time, when she was getting restraining orders, did she come and stay with you for any length of time?"

"No. She had her own apartment though. She maintained that apartment for many years. In fact, she still had her own separate apartment at the time she died."

"Did she explain to you why she got restraining orders against Mr. Porter?"

"Objection, hearsay."

"Sustained. Ms. Hughes, you have to find another way to establish why the victim in this case obtained restraining orders against Mr. Porter."

I knew that wouldn't be a problem. I was quite sure Ally had obtained a copy of the restraining orders, and they would be exceptions to the hearsay rule, as they were business records kept in the ordinary course of business. Assuming she produced these records in court, I wouldn't object to them being entered into evidence.

Sure enough, Ally produced a copy of both restraining orders. "I would like to enter these restraining orders, these orders of protection, into evidence."

"No objection," I said.

At that, Ally had the records marked as exhibits, and she passed them around to the jury. "I reserve the right to question the defendant about these restraining orders."

"Were you concerned for the safety of your daughter?"

She nodded. "I definitely was."

"Was there anything that happened recently that made you more concerned for her safety than you were before?"

"Yes. My daughter got engaged to a man by the name of David Taylor. She got engaged to him while Silas was away on a business trip in Europe. I was very concerned that when she told Silas she was leaving him for another man, he would harm her."

"I have nothing further for this witness."

Crap. Ally did not open the door for me to cross-examine Opal on the issue of the identical twin sisters. I decided to ask her the questions I needed to ask her anyways, hoping Ally would not object to my asking them. If she did, I would have to call Opal as my own witness and treat her as hostile.

I figured there was a good chance Ally would not object to my cross-examining Opal on issues not brought up in the direct examination. After all, she knew I would try to get this evidence from Opal one way or another. If she wanted a trial to not drag on forever, she would let me ask the questions I needed to ask.

I stood up and approached the witness. "Ms. Jackson, you stated on direct you saw bruises on the arms of your daughter. Yet you questioned your daughter on where she got those bruises, and she did not tell you my client was hitting her. Isn't that correct?"

She nodded. "Yes. That is correct."

"Were you aware your daughter was involved in an alternative lifestyle?"

"I don't know what you mean."

"I mean your daughter enjoyed being beaten by strangers. She was sexually gratified by strangers beating her. Were you aware she was involved in these kinds of activities?"

My strategy was to throw her off balance and hope she would mess up when I asked her about the identical twin situation.

She shook her head. "My word. No. I didn't realize people did things like that." She looked mortified. "Why would anybody be sexually gratified by being beaten?"

"There is an alternative lifestyle known as bondage discipline sadism and masochism. BDSM for short. Have you ever heard of the term BDSM?"

"Well I've heard of that book, that *50 Shades of Gray* book, but I didn't think people actually did that in real life. And I certainly never imagined my daughter was involved with something like that."

"Your daughter Ava has an identical twin, correct?" I looked over at Ally to see if she would object, but she didn't.

"Yes. She had an identical twin."

"And you stated on direct your daughter is engaged to a man by the name of David Taylor, and that was why you feared for her life. Isn't that right?"

"Yes. That is correct."

"And who is David Taylor currently engaged to?"

She shifted uncomfortably in her seat. "He's engaged to my daughter Emma."

I paced back and forth. "Emma. Is Emma the identical twin of Ava?"

"Yes. That is correct."

"And when did they get engaged?"

"They got engaged on June 1."

"June 1. And Ava was murdered on May 19. So, Ava is murdered on May 19, and not two weeks later, Emma is engaged to the man Ava was engaged to before her death. Isn't that right?"

"Emma and David were friends from way back. They knew each other for quite a long time. They leaned on each other after Ava died."

"And in fact, you held a large engagement party for David and Emma, didn't you? You held a party the first week of July. A large shindig at the Mission Hills Country Club, attended by 300 of her closest friends. Isn't that right?"

"Yes. Of course. We always hold parties for occasions such as engagements and weddings."

I paced back and forth. I was about ready to trap her. "I see. So, Emma and David got engaged on June 1, and one month later you held an event that was attended by 300 of her closest friends. This was on a Saturday night, wasn't it? During the summer, right?"

"Right. It was on a Saturday night and it was a very nice evening."

"The Mission Hills Country Club is not the kind of country club where you can hold an event with just a month's notice, is it? Especially during the summer time, when that country club is packed with different events, especially on the weekends. Isn't that right?"

I took a look at her face, and it dawned on her that she had fallen into a trap. "Well, no."

"As a matter of fact, to have an event such as the event you held for Emma and David, you would had to have booked the country club for at least a year in advance. Isn't that true?"

"There was a last-minute cancellation. We got lucky."

"Actually, there's a waiting list for these openings. You would not have been very high on the waiting list, considering you were trying to plan that event only a month in advance."

She didn't say anything. She knew she was lying and the jury also knew she was lying. There was no way she could've gotten a Saturday night event, during the summer, with only a month's notice. She knew it. She knew the jury knew it.

"Actually, you planned this engagement party much earlier, didn't you? In fact, you planned it a year ago. Isn't that right?"

She sighed. "Yes. That's true."

"In fact, you had actually planned this engagement party a year in advance, but the engagement party was originally supposed to be for Ava and David, isn't that true?"

She leaned closer into the microphone. She hesitated. "Yes. We planned the engagement party a year in advance, and it was originally supposed to be for Ava and David."

"I see. So your daughter Ava was brutally murdered on May 19 of this year, and two weeks later, David is engaged to Emma, Ava's identical twin, and on July 1, you hold a party for David and Emma, a party that was supposed to be for David and Ava. Isn't that right?"

"I know it seems insensitive, but we had the date all planned out, we had already paid for the party, so –"

"I see what you mean. I mean, after all, Ava certainly did not have a need for that party anymore, right? So why not just give Emma the party Ava was supposed to have with the man she was supposed to be with? I mean, after all, Ava had only been dead for a little over a month at that time. That's a good time to party, isn't it?"

She crossed her arms in front of her. "I don't know what you're getting at."

"I'll tell you what I'm getting at. Emma and David were not the ones who had that party, but, rather, it was Ava and David, wasn't it? That's because Emma is actually dead, as she was the one who died in my client's dungeon, not Ava. Isn't that right?"

She shook her head. She looked at Silas nervously. She looked very unsure.

"I'll remind you that you are under oath."

She finally took a deep breath. I knew she was trying to calculate if she should lie, knowing I would break down somebody somewhere along the line. She looked down at the stand. "No, that's not true."

"Oh, but it is true. It is true. Admit it. Admit that Emma was dying of pancreatic cancer, your daughter Ava made a deal with Emma, where Emma agreed to pose as Ava and consume the barbiturate known as Secobarbital, whereupon Ava would Emma's identity, because Ava wanted to get away from my client without him tracking her down. Emma was going die anyway, probably painfully. At least this way her death could mean something. It could mean freedom for Ava. Isn't that right?"

"No. That's not true." I could see by her face and her body language, however, that this was true. She couldn't look me in the eye. Her shoulders were hunched and she was slouched down.

"And you and your husband were in on the scheme. The two of you believed my client was abusing Ava and she wanted to get away from him. It was tragic your daughter was dying, but I'm sure Emma making the sacrifice for Ava made her death seem much more worthwhile. Isn't that right?"

"I said no."

"I have nothing further."

I sat down. I knew I had drawn a considerable amount of blood with that exchange. What parents would throw a party for their daughter, a party meant for their other brutally murdered daughter, just a little over a month after that murder?

"Counselor, do you have any redirect?" Judge Pruitt asked Ally.

"No Your Honor."

"The witness is excused. Ms. Hughes, call your next witness."

"The state calls David Taylor."

I would have to hammer him just the way I hammered Opal.

He was sworn in, and Ally got right to work. "Mr. Taylor, are you the fiancé of Emma Jackson?"

"Yes. I am."

"And were you the fiancé of Ava Porter?"

"Yes I was."

"And when did you and Ava Porter become engaged?"

"About a year ago. Ava was still living with Silas, but we were seeing each other behind his back for several months. He was away on business a lot. Then he left for six months for an extended business trip to Europe and Ava lived with me during that time."

"And were you concerned for the safety of Ava Porter?"

"Yes. I was."

"And why were you concerned for her safety?"

"I was concerned for her safety because she was

engaged to me and I knew he had abused her. And she was fearful of him. She was specifically afraid he would kill her once he found out she was engaged to me."

"I have nothing further for this witness."

I stood up. I felt David did not add much of anything to Ally's case, but he would be invaluable to mine. I thought Ally was strategically stupid for calling him in the first place.

"Mr. Taylor, you are currently engaged to Emma Jackson. Isn't that true?"

"Yes. That's true."

"Actually, that's not true, is it? You're actually still engaged to Ava Porter, isn't that true?"

As with Opal, he hesitated. It was as if he was turning the question around in his mind, trying to decide if he should answer truthfully or not. After all, he was under oath. He knew the truth. "No. That doesn't make sense. Ava is dead. She died in that guesthouse your client maintained. She died painfully in a fire."

"Is your father a scientist?"

"Yes. He is. He works for the federal government."

"And would he be able to get a hold of a barbiturate by the name of Secobarbital?"

"I suppose so. He is a chemist."

"Isn't it true you asked him for a vial of Secobarbital with the intention of giving it to Emma Jackson? And isn't it true your father gave it to you, and you gave that drug to Emma? Granted, Emma was in on the plan, but that's what happened, wasn't it?"

He crossed his arms in front of him. "No. That's not true."

"It's not? So are you testifying in open court that you're engaged to Ava Porter's identical twin, Emma Jackson, and you got engaged to her not even a month after Ava was killed? How were you able to move on so fast?"

"Emma and I have been close for years —"

"How were you and Emma so close for so many years when Emma had been living in Australia since the age of 20?" Anna had actually managed to find out that Emma had been living in Australia for the past 12 years. When I found out that Emma had actually moved to Australia when she was 20, it explained to me how Silas never knew about Emma's existence. I did not know what the circumstances were for Emma moving to Australia so many years before, but it was safe to assume she did not maintain contact with her family. It was also safe to assume she did not leave on good terms. In fact, she did not return to the United States until she got sick and sought treatment at the Mayo Clinic in Rochester, Minnesota.

"I —"

"In fact, Emma Jackson did not live in the United States until January of this year. And during that time, she was living in Minnesota, seeking treatment for pancreatic cancer. So tell me how you were able to get so close to Emma in such a short period of time?"

I threw him and I knew it. He shifted in his chair and then paused for a long time. "I guess Emma and I weren't really close for a long time. But, after Ava died, we became close. We became very close because we leaned on each other."

"You didn't address what I said earlier. I specifically stated that Emma was seeking treatment at the Mayo Clinic in Rochester, Minnesota, for pancreatic cancer. You did not refute that, so is it safe to say you agree she was seeking treatment for pancreatic cancer at the Mayo Clinic?"

He looked like he was about to panic. "I don't know

about that. I wasn't aware she was seeking treatment for pancreatic cancer."

"You weren't aware of this?" Once again, I laid a careful trap, and he fell right into it. His fiancée, the woman he was calling Emma Jackson, was as far from a pancreatic cancer patient as anybody could possibly be. If he was trying to say he had no clue that the healthy woman who the jury would soon see was seeking treatment for the most deadly kind of cancer there is, it was obvious he was lying. Any other man in his situation would say "what do you mean, she was seeking treatment for pancreatic cancer? There's nothing wrong with her. In fact she's very healthy." They certainly would not say, as David was saying, that they didn't know if their healthy fiancée was seeking treatment for pancreatic cancer.

"That's what I'm saying. I wasn't aware she was seeking treatment for pancreatic cancer."

"So then, what you're saying is you weren't aware she was seeking treatment for pancreatic cancer, but that it is a possibility she was seeking treatment for this. Is that what you're saying?"

He looked unsure. "That's what I'm saying."

"So does she show any signs of pancreatic cancer? Emma, does she show any signs she's dying?"

"No. In fact, she seems very healthy."

"In fact, she does seem very healthy. She's actually in very good shape, isn't she? She's very fit and energetic. Right?"

"Yes, that's right."

"Yet you admit that there's a possibility she was being treated for pancreatic cancer, the most deadly kind of cancer there is?"

"I guess so."

"I have nothing further for this witness."

I thought that exchange went well. As well as it possibly could.

But the person I was most looking forward to was the person scheduled to testify next.

The state was about to call Emma Jackson to the stand.

## Chapter Twenty-Seven

EMMA JACKSON, a.k.a. Ava Porter, approached the stand looking for all the world like she just came off the tennis court. She was tanned and wearing a short skirt and tight sweater. Her skirt showed off her gorgeous legs and tight rear end to their best effect. As before, she had apparently just gotten her nails done, and it looked like her hair was newly styled as well.

She walked rapidly to the stand and sat down.

She could not have known that it had come out in open court that she was possibly being treated for pancreatic cancer. She was out in the hallway when David was testifying, as I had invoked the rule on witnesses, which meant the witnesses could not be present in the courtroom when the other witnesses were testifying. I had brought out the fact that she was supposed to be sick with pancreatic cancer in when I was grilling David, and since he did not dispute her possible sickness, but admitted it was possible, I was eager to show to the jury just how healthy this woman was.

She was sworn in, and Ally started asking her questions. "Please state your name for the record."

She leaned close to the microphone. "Emma Jackson."

"And Miss Jackson, could you please tell the court how you are related to the victim in this case, Ava Porter?"

"I am her identical twin."

"And could you tell me if you believe the relationship between Mr. and Mrs. Porter was healthy or unhealthy?"

"It was definitely unhealthy."

"What do you know about the relationship between Mr. and Mrs. Porter?"

"I knew there were restraining orders. I knew about the bruises. And I knew my sister was going to leave Mr. Porter for David Taylor."

"Now, I understand you are currently engaged to Mr. Taylor. Is that true?"

"Yes. That's true."

"Can you tell the court how your relationship with Mr. Taylor began?"

I knew she would lie. I also knew she had no idea that David had admitted that Emma Jackson had not lived in town for many years, and she had just started living in the United States this past January. I was unclear as to when Emma started living in the Kansas City area, if she did at all.

"Well, he was a friend of the family for years and we grew up together. We've known each other for years. And when Ava died, we grew very close. We were both so sad and upset that we were drawn to each other, to lean on each other. And then it just happened. We fell in love. I don't think that anybody can begrudge us that – we found love in the middle of tragedy."

Oh, she was good. She had a little Kleenex and she kept

dabbing her eyes. "I'm so sorry, it just hurts so bad to even talk about her anymore. I loved her so much. And to have her die in such a way..." She shook her head. "I just can't imagine it. Dying at the hands of that monster. It just makes me sick."

"Were you concerned for Ava's safety?"

"Yes. I was. I was concerned for her safety because I knew she was engaged to David, and I did some research on battered women, and I found out that the most dangerous time for a battered woman is when she's getting ready to leave her abuser. So yes, I was very scared for her."

"I have nothing further for this witness."

Ally sat down, and I stood up. "Ms. Jackson, or should I say Mrs. Porter," I began.

She visibly bristled. She looked me right in the eye. "I know what you're getting at. For some odd reason you have this obsession with the fact I am not who I say I am. I don't know why you think I would ever, and I mean ever, take my sister's identity, but I will not answer to the name Mrs. Porter. I won't answer to the name Ava. I won't answer to either of those names, so I would ask you to address me by my name, Emma. Or Ms. Jackson is fine too." She sat up straighter in her chair and glared at me. Challenged me. The look in her eyes said *just try it. Just try to prove I took my sister's identity. You can't.*

I wouldn't accede her point. "If you aren't Ava Porter, then why were you willing to have an engagement party on July 1, an engagement party meant for Ava? This engagement party happened less than a month and 1/2 after your sister was allegedly brutally murdered. So you're telling the court to believe that you would be willing to take your murdered sister's party, after taking your murdered sister's fiancé? The same murdered sister who you allegedly loved so much, and whose death made you so sad and depressed. Is that what you're willing to tell the court?"

"Mr. Harrington, I don't know why you're judging me. The heart wants what it wants. As for my taking her engagement party, that's a lie. My parents managed to plan this party after David and I got engaged. We got engaged on June 1, and my parents were able to quickly plan a party, and the party took place on July 1."

I shook my head and wagged my finger at her. "That isn't what your mother said on the stand when she testified. She testified the party that took place on July 1 was originally a party planned for Ava and David. She admitted that it was impossible to book a party at the Mission Hills Country Club on a Saturday night in the summertime with just a month's lead time. So now you are lying under oath. Its obvious to the court that you are lying."

She shot daggers at me through her eyes. She had no idea her mother had come clean on the stand about whose party that really was, so she had no idea she was caught in a lie. "Okay. Yes, that engagement party was originally for my sister and David. So what? We already had the deposits made on the party, already had the menu planned, already had the space, already had the guest list. So we didn't want to cancel the party. We didn't want to let everybody down. So yes. David and I went ahead and had a party meant for him and Ava. I wasn't aware that was a crime." She crossed her arms in front of her and glared at me with a pissed-off look.

"No, it is not a crime to take a party meant for your sister. That's not a crime. But it is a crime to assume her identity – that is a crime."

"I do agree that would be a crime if that's what happened, but that's not what happened."

"It would also be a crime to kill your sister and take her identity. And that's what happened here, wasn't it? You gave your sister poison, while she was posing as you, and you timed it so you would know when she would die. Then when she died, you set the dungeon on fire with an accelerant, so your sister's remains couldn't be identified properly and the fact that the drug known as Secobarbital was in her system would be missed by the medical examiner. And that's also an important point – where would my client get ahold of Secobarbital? He wouldn't be able to, but you would be able to – through David's father, wouldn't you?"

She shook her head. "That's a great imagination you have there."

"Emma was dying, wasn't she? She was dying of pancreatic cancer."

As I crossed her, she kept shaking her head desperately.

"She was dying of pancreatic cancer, and the two of you never got along. Isn't that right?"

"No. That's not right. We were very close."

"If the two of you were so close, then why is it that my client, Silas Porter, never knew his wife Ava had an identical twin? Why is it he never met Emma Jackson? Ava and Silas were married for seven years, but he never met Emma. Never even heard of her. Now if you were so close with her sister, why is it that Silas never knew she existed?"

"I don't know why he never knew she existed."

I smiled. "Don't you mean you don't know why he never knew why *you* existed?"

She looked confused. "That's what I just said. I just said I didn't know why he never knew why I existed."

"Actually, no. You said, and I quote, I don't know why he never knew she existed. *She* existed."

I looked over to the judge. "Could you please have the

court reporter read back the witness' response to my question about why Silas never knew she existed?"

Judge Pruitt looked over at the court reporter. "Could you please read back the witness' response to that question?"

The court reporter looked at her transcript. "I don't know why he never knew she existed."

I turned back to her. "You know what the definition of a gaffe is, don't you? It's when you accidentally tell the truth."

She glared at me. I caught her, and she knew it. She just stared at me for several minutes. You could hear a pin drop in the courtroom as she glared at me, not saying a word. She took several deep breaths and sighed several times. It was only a matter of time before she had to come clean, and I knew it would happen sooner or later.

Turned out it was sooner, rather than later. "Okay. Okay. You got me. Yes, Ava was not the person who died in that dungeon. It was my sister, Emma. And yes, she was dying of pancreatic cancer. Have you ever seen anybody slowly die of cancer? I'll give you a hint. It's not like in the movies." She looked away. "It's painful. People don't look beautiful as they die like you see in the movies. They lose their hair, they lose their body, they have to go and have fluid drained from their belly all the time. If they want to live longer, they have to take chemotherapy that makes them sicker. Chemotherapy kills all cells, not just cancer cells, so the final months of your life are spent puking your guts out, laying on the bathroom floor, wanting to die. Your organs fail, one by one. At some point, you just close your eyes and don't wake up. But it takes days for you to die that way."

I decided to just let her continue on.

"So she wanted me to help her die. She begged me to

help her die. She told me I owed her that." More glaring at me, but she was on a roll. "You're right, we never got along. I hated her because she stole my husband when we were 20 years old. She moved to Australia with Chris, my husband, and shunned all of us. I turned our parents against her, and she's been dead to me all these years."

"So I agreed to help her die. We reconciled our differences, and she decided," she said. "She decided, not me, to make her death mean something. She came up with the idea to take poison and pose as me so Silas would be nabbed for her murder."

"And why did the two of you cook this plan up?"

"Because. I wanted to get away from Silas, and I knew he would never leave me alone. Ever. I tried to leave him several times, years ago, and he stalked me and made my life hell. He followed me, wherever I went, and would just appear out of nowhere whenever I was on a date with somebody new. He told me, in no uncertain terms, that he would haunt me until the day I died if I decided to leave him. He called me constantly, and, you have to understand, he's a very wealthy and powerful man. If I left him and moved to Siberia, he would find me. He told me as much. So, yes, I had to do something drastic. Emma agreed to help me."

I had to smile. I just won. "What about the fire? How did that happen?"

She shook her head. "That's how we planned it. I was right outside the dungeon, listening and watching the two of them. That's how we planned it – after she died, I was to set fire to the dungeon."

She was still staring at me with her head held high.

"I have nothing further for this witness."

"Ms. Hughes, do you have any redirect for this witness?"

Ally stood up. "No, Your Honor." She looked at me. "I would like to ask for a short recess."

"The witness is excused. However, I would like to ask the bailiff to take the witness into custody. Let's everybody take a five minute break."

The jury filed out, the bailiff took Ava into custody, and the judge addressed us. "Well, looks like your case just fell apart," he said to Ally. "Right before your eyes."

Ally shook her head. "Looks like it."

"I expect you to dismiss it when the jury gets back," Judge Pruitt said.

Ally sighed. "I will."

"Good."

She turned to me. "I just can't believe that happened. What just happened?"

"You need to listen to me more often," I said. "I told you. You never listen."

"Man, people are psycho. They'll do anything, won't they?"

"You know it. I've always known it. Looks like you're learning it too."

The jury came back in, Ally dismissed the case, and it was over.

This might have been over, but I had something much more pressing to worry about.

Nate.

## Chapter Twenty-Eight

I WAS RELIEVED the trial was over so soon. I was surprised about the way it ended. Nobody was more surprised than me. Harper couldn't stop laughing about it all. "You're a regular Perry Mason," she had said. "Breaking her down on the stand like that."

"Well," I said, "I tripped her up, and that was that. She knew I had her when she said, accidentally, she didn't know why Silas didn't know about *her,* when she clearly should have said *me.* Plus, her mother was stupid, trying to make the court believe she just planned that huge Mission Hills Country Club shindig in a month. Everybody knows that's not possible on a Saturday night in the summertime at a popular country club like that one. Then, when Ava tried to parrot that same line, and I told her her mother already told the truth, I knew she was breaking. It's hard, or it must be hard, to keep up such a lie."

But I needed to spend some time with Nate. That was important to me. Gretchen was watching him, but I hadn't had the chance to really talk to him since he admitted to me his teacher had been molesting him.

I got home and went right up to Nate's room. He was laying on the bed, reading a magazine. "Hey Dad," he said. "How was your trial?"

I went over and sat on the end of his bed. "It went well. We won." I took a deep breath. "That's all well and good, but it's not what really matters to me. I like winning cases, but what really matters to me is you and your sister. If you guys are hurting, nothing else really matters to me but to make it all better. I don't know how I can possibly make this all better, but I'm gonna try."

He shrugged. "Mrs. Bowen helped me when I thought nobody was around for me. Amelia was sick, Mom was gone, and you were always at the hospital with Amelia, or taking her to the doctor, or just worrying about her. It seemed like you didn't even know I existed. I was trying to deal with my mom being gone, and I thought Amelia would die, and I just didn't know what was going on. So I talked to Mrs. Bowen about what was going on. She helped me." He hung his head. "I don't hate her. I think she's very sad. I don't want her to go to prison. I never wanted any of this to happen."

I put my hand on his shoulder. "You were very brave to tell me about what she was doing to you. I just wish you would've come to me before it came to you taking a gun to school."

"I wouldn't use it. I just wanted to somebody to hear me. I felt like I was invisible. I just wanted to be visible again."

Nate was breaking my heart. I knew he was right – I had been very preoccupied for the past few years. How could I not be? Amelia got sick, and I thought she would die. She got well, then I was charged with my father's murder while Sarah was threatening to terminate the parental rights to my own daughter. Then I had to deal with the fallout from that, as Amelia found out she was not my biological daughter. So I had to make sure we were good – Amelia and me. Through all this, I was maintaining a full-time job, with lots of high-profile cases to try. I realized I had prioritized Amelia first, myself and my murder charge second, my job third, and Nate was an afterthought.

Nate was an afterthought. And he knew it. He was a kid – kids always know much more than we think they know. They usually knew more than the adults. How could Nate not know he was such a low priority to me? I was so blind that I had no clue he was hurting. I mean, I kind of knew he was hurting, but I didn't know what to do about it, so I just ignored it.

I ignored him.

I swallowed hard. "Nate, I want you to know something. You're very important to me. I know that for the past few years, things have been crazy. It hasn't been your fault at all. It hasn't been my fault either - at least it wasn't my fault that Amelia got sick, I was charged with murdering my father, and then Sarah let Amelia know I'm not her biological dad. None of that was my fault, and it wasn't your fault either. But I was completely at fault for not prioritizing you and your needs. I know it has not been easy for you, seeing your sister get so sick, seeing me going through that whole investigation about my father's murder, seeing your mother take off without a word, and seeing your mother not wanting to have anything to do with you or your sister. I haven't provided the most stable environment for you. I haven't been a good father to you. I want to change that. I want to do all I can to make sure you know how important you are to me."

He nodded. "I'd like that, Dad." He hung his head and then looked at me shyly through his bangs. "Is Mom really gone? Is she never coming back?"

"I'm afraid she's gone. I've talked to her about spending time with you guys, but she has her own life now. I'm so sorry, but I think it's just you and me, kid. You, me, and Amelia. It's just the three of us."

I saw tears come to his eyes and I put my arms around him and hugged him tight. He cried on my shoulder for what seemed like forever. I felt his pain. My heart was breaking, but there wasn't much I could do.

All I could do was hold him while he cried, and try to make good on my vow to be a better father for him.

---

THAT NIGHT, after Nate and I talked for several hours, he went to bed, and I had the guys over. I tried to see them every couple of weeks, to see how they were doing, and make sure I kept up on their lives. I had put them on the back-burner too, because my life had been so crazy, but they understood.

I was working with Nick and Jack. They both were working with Tom Garrett doing investigations for Harper and me. Tommy was working construction and Connor was still in school, working toward his social work degree.

The guys came over, bringing a 12-pack of beer. We sat on my porch, drinking beers and watching the fireflies. It was an unseasonably hot October evening, and if it weren't for the fact that I had a long road ahead with Nate, I probably would've felt extremely happy. I won my trial. I was a free man, and that was not at all a sure thing after I was arrested for murdering my dad. Ally and I were getting along well, Amelia was healthy and we had gotten past the whole issue about her not being my biological daughter.

Life should have been good, but it wasn't. There was always something to worry about, and, at the moment, I was very worried about Nate. I wondered if the damage was done and there was no coming back. I wondered if he would end up like me, hating the world and wreaking havoc on those around him. I would do all I could to make sure that didn't happen, but what if it was out of my control? What if Nate was more deeply troubled than anybody knew?

"Buddy," Tommy said, when I told the guys about my talk with Nate. "Get on top of that shit. You can't let him go down the same path we all did."

I nodded. "I am going to get on top of it, but how? I have an appointment with a therapist for him, the same therapist who has been our family therapist, but who knows if it's going to do the trick."

Connor, the most sensitive of the bunch, took a sip of his beer and put his arm around me. "You'll figure it out. You've always been the smartest one out of all of us."

"Low bar to clear there," Nick said with a laugh. "But you're right, Connor. Damien has always been the smart one. Damien, I wish we all had a magic bullet, but we don't. I guess you'll have to play it by ear. Lock up your gun, do all you can to make sure Nate stays at that school, because the last thing you want to do is uproot him when he's already having problems, make sure that Mrs. Bowen stays the fuck away from him, and try to pay more attention to the poor kid. He's got whiplash, that's all. He'll be fine, but only if you make sure he is."

I stared at the fireflies while I continued to sip my beer. "You know, when I got out of the joint, and got my law degree at The University of Chicago, I thought I was on my way. I thought life had cleared a path for me. The worst was over. I had Sarah, I had two healthy kids, I had my freedom, and I had a bright future. All that shit happened to me, being wrongfully imprisoned, killing my stepfather, all of that, and I goddamned made it through in one piece." I shook my head. "What happened? How did it all fall apart again? Why wasn't my path cleared like I thought it was?"

It was Jack's turn to give advice. "It's life, buddy. Life. It'll hit you with a 2 x 4 just when you aren't ready. Just when you think you have it all figured out, life will knock you on your ass every damn time. You just have to get back up every time. You never have it made, and the second you think you do, you'll find out just how full of shit you were for ever thinking that."

I took a deep breath. "You guys ever think about how lucky we all are to not be in prison? I guess I need to look at it that way. Any day I have my freedom is a good one. No matter what happens."

We all took another sip and silently listened to the sounds of distant cars and barking dogs, and watched the fireflies slowly fade with the night, as the sun was starting to come up. It had been a long time since I stayed up all night with the guys, just shooting the shit, but I think they knew I needed the company.

They finally left, and I went up to Nate's room and watched him sleep. It was around 5 AM, and he didn't need to be in school, so I would let him sleep in.

He lost his innocence already, at the age of 10.

But if it were possible to lose your innocence when bad things start to happen and your parent ignores you when your world is turning upside down, I realized Nate probably lost his innocence long ago.

And that fucking broke my heart.

## Chapter Twenty-Nine

### April 1 - this year

"HELLO, EMMA," Ava Porter said to her sister. "I guess the prodigal daughter has finally returned." She raised her eyebrow at the identical twin sister who she hadn't seen in some 12 years. Ever since Emma seduced Ava's husband and ran off with him to Australia, the two hadn't spoken. The fact that Emma not only did that, but also cut off all contact with the family meant that, for all intents and purposes, Emma had been dead to the family all these years.

Ava crossed her arms, but she felt slightly concerned about her twin sister. Emma wasn't looking well. At all. She was super-skinny and her skin didn't look right. Her eyeballs were yellow, and her skin had a slightly yellow hue as well.

"Ava," Emma said. "I'm back in the states."

"I see that." Ava still was standing in front of Emma, her arms still crossed in front of her defensively. "What's up with that Australian accent? It's totally fake, just like you've always been."

"I've been living in Brisbane for 12 years," Emma said. "I picked it up, so sue me." Emma's defensiveness echoed Ava's own. "I told you I was sorry about Christopher."

"Oh, no. No you didn't. You were more 'sorry, not sorry,' than genuinely sorry. By the way, I found out that Chris left you for another woman. All I can say is karma."

Emma shook her head. "Maybe I didn't apologize properly, but I really did feel shame for what I did. Not to mention embarrassment. He really was a wanker, as it turned out, but I was so embarrassed about his leaving me, and I didn't want to hear 'I told you so' from all of you, so I just dropped off the face of the earth. I did, and that wasn't fair."

"Damned right, that wasn't fair." Ava took a deep breath. "But you're here now, so…"

Emma nodded. "I'm here in the states, because I'm seeing a doctor at the Mayo Clinic." She hesitated and her hand fluttered to her hair. "A wig," she said, pointing to her blonde bob. "It looks pretty natural, doesn't it?"

Ava narrowed her eyes and put her hand on her sister's hair. "Why do you need a wig?" she asked suspiciously.

Emma swallowed hard. "I'm dying. Pancreatic cancer."

Ava's eyes got wide and she touched her mouth in shock. "Emma, if this is an April Fool's Joke, it's not funny. Not even funny." Emma was always a prankster when the two twins were growing up together. But this was one prank that Ava did not find humorous at all.

Emma shook her head. "I wish it were a joke, sis, but it's not. I haven't been feeling well for several months. Just rundown, no appetite. I went to see doctor after doctor. Gall stones, they said. Gastritis, they said. I had my gallbladder taken out, had exploratory surgery, and nobody could find a thing. I finally got my diagnosis last month, and I've been seeking treatment in Minnesota at the Mayo Clinic. There's not much they can do, though. With chemo, I can live maybe a year. Without it…" She shook her head again. "I could be dead next week."

The news hit Ava like a ton of bricks. "No." She shook her head. "No. That's not fair. I always assumed you and I would be close again, like we were when we were kids. I thought we had time to become twins again. Please say you're just playing a really sick joke on me. Please…"

"I wish I were joking. More than you can ever know. But I'm not. I'm at peace with it, but I need you to help me. I know I haven't earned your help or your compassion, but I don't have much time. I would love your assistance in helping me die."

"No. I can't do that. I can't-"

Emma put her hands on Ava's shoulders. "We need to talk about this more. I just wanted to throw it out to you."

---

THE TWO TWINS spent several days together, bonding and reminiscing about good times. It was time to make amends, and Emma knew it. Ava did, as well.

But, after several days, Emma started to vomit pure blood, and Ava suddenly saw just how serious her sister's condition was. By then, Emma had found out just how toxic Ava's relationship was with her husband, and just how much Ava was nervous that Silas would stalk her and not leave her alone.

"It was terrible," Ava said. "When I left him, he was

calling me and texting me constantly. He somehow always found out where I was. He tracked me down through my phone, but I got a new phone, and he still would show up at any restaurant I was at. He started fights with my dates all the time, and, by the end of the evening, my date would inform me that he didn't want to get involved with the drama."

"Was he physical with you?"

Ava shook her head. "Twice, he was. He beat me twice. I called the cops both times, but he was never arrested. He has more money than God, and he's very powerful." She sighed. "I don't know, Emma. I just don't think I'll ever be able to get away from him. And I need to get away from him. I've fallen in love with a golf pro at the country club. His name is David Taylor, and, Emma, he's the one. Finally, I found somebody to really love. But I just think Silas won't ever leave us alone. He won't let us have any peace. I just know it."

Emma nodded slowly. "I have an idea. If it works, you'll be rid of Silas for good."

"What's your idea?"

"Well, I want you to help me die. Can you possibly get your hands on some Secobarbital?"

"Emma-"

"Ava, please. My vomiting blood yesterday was only the beginning. I'm constantly in excruciating pain. Constantly nauseous. I have to go to the doctor every few days to have fluid drained off my abdomen. It's only going to get worse from here. I don't have a chance to live, Ava. No chance at all. Please, hear me out."

Ava sat there, waiting for Emma to continue. "I don't want to do this…"

"Please. Secobarbital is a barbiturate that will help me just go to sleep and never wake up. What if I took a lethal dose, and I took your place and somehow, someway, my death would result in Silas' being tried for murder? Your murder."

"I-"

"My death could mean something if I could help you. Let me help you."

"Let's not talk about this."

"Ava, don't avoid this. Don't avoid it. I owe you something. I stole your husband and I dropped off the face of the earth. I could help you get rid of Silas for good."

Ava shook her head. "No."

---

TWO DAYS LATER, Ava came around. "Okay. Here's what you can do. Silas and I are into bondage games. You can pose as me. What if I gave you enough of a dose of a barbiturate that you pass away while he's having sex with you? You can take the drug, then ask him to put a bag over your head. That's something we do all the time. I read about it on the Internet - the combination of a lethal dose of barbiturates and slipping a plastic bag over your head will bring about death. I'll be outside the dungeon, listening and watching, and, when I know you've died, I'll set a wildfire with an accelerant, which will burn your body to the extent that the medical examiner won't be able to identify the true cause of death and she won't be able to ever ascertain it was you who died and not me."

Emma was nervous about the idea, but it sounded foolproof. "As long as you are certain I have died before you set that fire, I will do it."

And their plan was hatched.
A perfect murder.
But not nearly as perfect as Ava had hoped for.

# Chapter Thirty

Two months later

SILAS NERVOUSLY APPROACHED the dilapidated home in South Kansas City. This was something he had meant to do for many years, but something always held him back.

It was irrational for him to hate his parents. A part of him always knew that. Yes, they sent him away at the age of 15 to go live in the UMKC dorm. They couldn't have possibly known how rejected that made him feel. All he wanted was for his adoptive parents to love him, but he knew he was a handful and, looking back, he couldn't really blame them for sending him away. After all, he was involved in many burglaries when he was very young, although he was never caught for any of it. He also set fires in other neighborhoods.

He was an angry kid. A very angry kid. His father killed his mother, violently and in a fire, and he tried to pin that fire on him, even though he was only 5 years old at the time. His biological mother never held him, never rocked him, never read to him. She ignored him, even when he was a tiny baby. He couldn't remember any of that, but his therapist uncovered it when he was put under hypnosis, and she diagnosed him with attachment disorder.

His biological mother rejected him, and then his adoptive parents also rejected him when they sent him away. And he vowed, then and there, he was done with them. Done. They rejected him, so he rejected them right back.

Yes, his adoptive mother and father went to see him all the time at the dorm. He was able to put on a happy face for them, but he secretly hated them both. He smiled to their faces, took his mother's cake and cookies and care packages, and then threw all of it in the trash when they left.

Then he left for Stanford for his PhD and never spoke with his parents again. They called and wrote constantly, but he never replied to any of it. They were dead to him.

Now, here he was. At his parents' house. It was his brush with prison time that finally made him realize he needed to make amends. He also had dreams, vivid dreams, that brought about the secret guilt eating away at him. Guilt about how he treated his adoptive parents.

His therapist told him his guilt was a healthy sign. It was a sign that maybe all of those intensive therapy sessions might have finally shifted something in him. He had been diagnosed with narcissistic personality disorder, and he intellectually knew that this personality disorder, as with all personality disorders, was not generally amenable to therapy. He still tried therapy, constantly, because he really wanted to get better.

His therapist informed him that true narcissists were unable to feel genuine guilt, so the fact that he was feeling guilty about how he treated his adoptive mother and father was a sign he had hope. He might be able to become normal yet.

He had a long way to go. He knew that. But this was a step forward.

He knocked on the door and his mother answered it. She looked almost the same as he remembered. Older, much older, and sadder. But she was still the mother he remembered from his youth.

"Hello, Mom," he said to the very startled Arlene.

She put her hand to her chest and her eyes got wide. "Silas?"

He nodded. "May I come in?"

"Of course, of course," she said. "Come on in." Then she turned her head. "Bob, come and see. Silas is here."

"Who?"

"Silas. Our son."

Silas stepped into the house and looked around. He smiled, because he knew he had a big surprise in store for his parents. They were surprised enough that he was even there at all. But when they saw what else he had in store for them, they would really be shocked. In a good way, of course.

Shocked in the best way.

The three of them stood awkwardly in the doorway for a few minutes. Then his mother finally got it together. "Well, please sit down." Then she went into the kitchen. "Gosh, I don't have much in the house to feed you. I always like to offer food to guests, but I just haven't gone shopping lately. Isn't that funny, though, I mean I work at Walmart. But I just haven't brought home groceries for awhile."

She finally brought out some bologna on white bread. "Here," she said. "I'm embarrassed I don't have something better."

Silas politely took a bite of the sandwich and smiled. "It's fine, Mom."

"So, what brings you here, son?" his father asked him. "I have to say, I thought we'd never see you again."

"I know. I'm here because I want to re-establish a relationship with the two of you. And I wanted to make amends for my years of neglect."

His mother nodded rapidly. "Oh, of course, of course. I always hoped and prayed to God that you would come back. I never gave up hope. I love you very much, Silas. You're our son. You will always be our son."

Silas smiled as he bent down to hug his mother. His father stood back for a few minutes, but then he, too, came over for a hug.

"Your mother is right. You're our son. You will always be our son. We want a relationship with you. That's all we've ever wanted."

Silas stood up. "Well, don't just stand there. Let's go and see what I have for the two of you. What I bought for the two of you."

His mother shook her head. "You don't owe us anything."

"I do. You two saved me from foster care. You saved me, and look how I've treated you." He motioned them outside. "Come on, get in the car. I'm going to take you to see something."

Bob and Arlene unsurely followed Silas to his car and got in. "Where are you taking us?"

"You'll see," Silas said with a smile.

Once they were all in the car, his father asked him about his murder case. "I saw in the paper you beat that murder case. Something about your wife sending in her identical twin to die in her place, and then framing you."

He shook his head. "What a nut. What happened to her, anyhow?"

"She pled guilty already and is on her way to prison for arson and second-degree murder. She's serving 20 years to life, but I have a feeling she'll be out before she's sixty." A part of him felt sorry for the woman. She did all that to him because he was a crazy stalker. And he *was* a crazy stalker. He knew he was. His bi-polar meds had helped him, though, and he no longer felt the obsessive tendencies he had felt back when he stalked his wife after she left him all those years ago.

He drove to his neighborhood with his parents, where he had bought a new house for them. It was a fully furnished, three-bedroom home with sparkling hardwood floors, luxury bathrooms with sunken jacuzzi tubs, a garden out back, a fireplace in both the living room and the den, and walk-in closets bigger than his parents' bedroom in that old dilapidated home.

The furniture he bought for them consisted of a matching leather couch and love-seat, two brand-new recliners, a large black marble dining room table with six cushioned chairs and a brand-new bed and cherry-wood dresser in the master bedroom.

As they walked in, his parents smiled. "Is this your home? It's beautiful," his mother said. She immediately walked to the sliding-glass door that looked out into the backyard. "What a beautiful garden," she said, "and bird-feeder." She walked into the yard, looking at the flowers, the fountains and the trees with wonder.

Silas knew his mother loved nature and would spend an endless amount of time in that garden, cultivating the flowers and plants with care.

As for his father, he bought him a 1957 Chevrolet Bel-

Air. It needed a lot of work, and that was by design. It was always his father's dream to restore a '57 Chevy, so Silas made sure the car he bought his father was one his father could work hard in restoring.

He showed his father the car.

"Beautiful, son," his father said with a whistle. "Just beautiful."

His mother came into the garage. "Look at that car," she said. "That's the kind of car you love, Bob."

"I know."

At that, Silas smiled broadly. "All this is yours, Mom and Dad. This house, the garden, this car, the furniture. Everything. I'm also going to make sure that neither of you have to work another day in your life. You need to be able to retire, Mom and Dad. Really retire."

His mother and father just stared at him in shock.

"I don't know what to say," his mother said.

"Just say you forgive me and you'll let me be your son again. That's all I want."

His mother started to cry, and, to his surprise, his father cried, too. "You didn't have to do this," his father said.

"Oh, but I did. I did."

Arlene and Bob went over and hugged Silas, and, as they all embraced, Silas felt something he had never felt before in his life.

He felt a sense of peace.

Next in the Kansas City
Legal Thrillers series

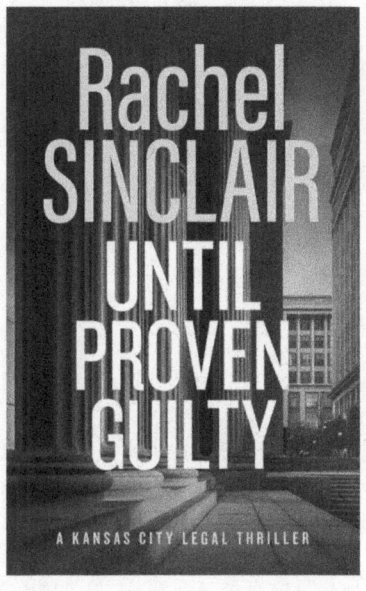

vinci-books.com/provenguilt

**With his son on the brink and his mother facing a murder accusation, Damien must expose the truth and save his family.**

Damien fights to clear his mother's name in a murder case that's anything but simple. As he unravels the mystery surrounding Dr. Tracy Dunham's death, Damien discovers a plot that puts his entire family at risk. With his son on the brink of self-destruction and powerful enemies closing in, Damien must race against time to expose the truth and save those he loves.

Turn the page for a free preview…

## Until Proven Guilty: Chapter One

"NOW, what is it that you suggest I do with Nate?" I asked my therapist, whose name was Dr. Betty Jordan. I had managed to talk Nate's school into letting him stay, even after he was caught with a gun in school, on the condition that he completed 40 hours of family therapy with an approved guidance counselor. Nate's school selected Dr. Jordan as the proper counselor, and Nate and I had been seeing her twice a week every week for the past six weeks. Nate had opened up to her, when she saw him individually, about what his teacher had done to him. Mrs. Bowen, his fifth-grade teacher, had pled guilty to molesting Nate and was awaiting sentencing at the moment.

"You really need to spend more time with him. I've spoken at length with both you and Nate, over the past six weeks, and what I'm getting from Nate is that he is a very isolated and lonely child. He feels neglected. He feels like he doesn't have any parents. Losing his mother has been very hard on him. But even more difficult for him is the thought that you don't care about him either. That's been very apparent to me."

I nodded. "I know what you're saying, but I don't realistically know if I can spend as much time with him as what I need to. I've already cut back my hours at work to deal with this, and I've tried to show Nate in every way possible that he's very important to me. I just don't know what more I can do."

Dr. Jordan just watched me. She had to have known what kind of predicament I was in. I was in a stressful position. A stressful profession. I had gone through the ringer myself in the past few years. Between having my wife running off on me, and having her tell my daughter that I was not her biological father, and the fact that I was on trial for my life after my biological father was found murdered and I was accused of it, I had been through it all in the past few years. All sorts of issues came up during my murder trial, including the fact that I had killed my stepfather when I was only 15 years old. I was never prosecuted for it, because he was going to kill either me or my mother or both of us, and he promised this all the time. Even as a kid, I knew it was his life or ours, and I chose his life.

The upshot was that the past few years had been beyond chaotic. My daughter Amelia had beaten cancer, but it was touch and go for a long time. There were years I didn't know if she would live to see her $10^{th}$ birthday. The bone marrow transplant finally was the thing that put her into remission, but, even now, I felt like her condition was touch and go. Her remission was precarious, as all remissions are, and she was not out of the woods. She was relatively healthy, thank God, but who knew how long that would last? Every time she got as much as a cold, I worried about her.

Amelia's sickness was just one more thing on my plate, and I didn't have the mental energy to really deal with my one healthy child. I was guilty of thinking he would just be okay because there was nothing obviously wrong with him. Of course, I was proved wrong, when he brought a gun into the school and aimed it at a kid who had been teasing him about being gay. He wasn't gay, at least not that I knew, but that was beside the point. That kid thought he was gay, and that was enough for him to bully Nate.

"You can take a leave of absence. Just until we manage to find the proper medication for your son and his signs of depression are lessened."

That was another thing I would have to deal with. The doctor wanted Nate on antidepressants. I was against it, as I was against all forms of medications, yet the doctor had been persistent that Nate needed some kind of antidepressants. She told me that if I didn't go along with her recommendations, she would not sign off to the school that we completed the requisite counseling. Which meant Nate might still end up being expelled from school. In other words, I needed to dance to her tune or Nate would suffer.

The doctor told me that giving anti-depressants to a child as young as Nate, a child who had just turned 11, was tricky, to say the very least. She reviewed all the side effects with me, including the fact that Nate might become suicidal, and I was dead set against it. I had to battle my own bouts of depression over my life and I always managed to get over it without drugs. I wanted Nate to do the same. Yet I gave in, just because of the threat that Nate might be expelled from school if I refused the doctor's recommendations. For a child in such a precarious and unstable position as Nate, being expelled from school would be the last straw for him. It would only be a matter of time before he went the way I went and ended up in prison. Staying in his school was his only hope of beating that scenario. I would do everything in my power to make sure he stayed at Pembroke Hill, the private school he attended.

Now the shrink wanted me to take a leave of absence. I could afford to take one, because I settled a personal injury case case years back that netted me $4 million. So financially, it wasn't a problem to take a long break from work. I just didn't want to leave Harper high and dry, as I had just become a partner in the law firm. She had a lot of cases on her plate and needed my help with them. The only other attorney in her office was named Tammy, an estate attorney who never appeared in court.

"Okay," I said reluctantly. "I guess I could take a small leave of absence. A sabbatical." My plan at that time was to take a leave of absence long enough to be home with Nate while he was going through the early stages of taking his antidepressants. It would apparently take some tweaking to find the right formula for him, as it always took a lot of tweaking to find the right formula for anybody. Because everybody's body chemistry was different, doctors always had to try different dosages and different drugs in different combinations to find out just the right combination and dosage of drugs to alleviate depression in any given person. Then they usually had to do some more tweaking later on, because meds tend to stop working after a certain period, so it would be back to the drawing board. Because Nate was so young, it was even trickier. There was a real chance he could become suicidal because of the antidepressants. That was a known risk. I certainly could not take the chance and leave Nate to his own devices when he was first taking these drugs.

But, as I left Dr. Jordan's office, I got a phone call that changed everything.

"Damien," my mom's voice was on the other end of the line. "I'm in the clink. The hoosegow. Gotta come down."

I rolled my eyes. This was not the first time my mother had been in the jail and it probably wouldn't be the last. My mother was regularly being taken to jail for one reason or another. Unpaid parking tickets, unpaid moving violations, a DUI or two. Always minor things, never anything enormous, unless you consider drunk driving to be enormous. That was just a routine thing for her anymore. I was really in no mood to have to deal with her. Not at that moment, when I was coming out of the therapist's office, with Nate strongly on my mind.

"I'll get there when I get there." That was a game we played. She would go to jail for one reason or another and I would take my own sweet time getting her out. That was my way of saying, in a very passive-aggressive way, that she needed to get her shit together. "What are you charged with this time? How many speeding tickets have you not paid, or maybe you got a DUI?"

"I wouldn't be making so much fun if I were you," she said. "I'm being charged with murder."

## Until Proven Guilty: Chapter Two

"COME AGAIN? Mom, seriously, this isn't funny."

"You think I'm being funny? I'll show you funny. Unless you think the cops coming into my house at 2 o'clock this morning and hauling my candied ass to jail, asking me all kinds of questions for the past 10 hours, if you think that's my idea of a good time, you got another thing coming. Now get down here. I didn't want to call you but the person I usually call to get me out of these things is deader than a doornail. And the cops think I'm the one who killed him."

I took a deep breath. "Mom, you're going to have to slow down. Who do they think you killed, and what –"

"They think I killed my friend Tracy Dunham. He's a guy I screw around with once in a while, good guy. Ain't never been more then a bed buddy, but we hang out too. Tracy, he was taking the drugs, which ain't no concern of mine. I don't get into that crap, but to each his own. Anyhow, turns out he's married. Or he was married, he ain't married now to nobody. He was married and his old lady threw him out of the house."

Mom was rambling, like she does, and I just had to let her do it.

"Last July, he comes over to my house, higher than a kite," Mom went on. "Tells me his bitch wife don't want him no more, can he crash? I say yeah, sure, why not? So he comes over and sleeps on my couch. I go to bed, I wake up and he's dead. You know, I try to do CPR and shit like that, I don't even know it all that well, but I seen it on TV shows. I try doing what I saw on TV. But he was stiff and cold, there ain't no bringing him back at that point. I didn't know what to do, so I call up the hospital, 911, they send somebody out to pick him up. They send the ambulance over and some woman, she says her job is to comfort the people who wake up to find a stiff in their house. I tell her I didn't need no comforting, I barely knew this guy, I wasn't shedding no tears for him. The cops come next, they question me, they want to do a piss test. I tell them okay, sure, why not? I ain't taking drugs. They're gonna find out I was drinking, but that ain't illegal, and I was sitting in my home, so I'm allowed to drink. They do a piss test, but they're not telling me the results."

She was on a roll, so I let her keep talking.

"They go into my medicine cabinet, I guess they figured out Tracy died of an overdose, they're looking in my medicine cabinet to see if I got some horse in there. I tell them 'have at it, knock yourself out, loser,' then they come out and tell me they're taking one of my BP meds in for testing. They tell me they found a suspicious powder in my BP med bottle.

They take him away, I think that's it, then two cops show up at my door three months later. They're telling me I'm responsible for Terry's death. They're saying they did an autopsy and some kind of test, toxic test or something like that, and-"

"Toxicology test," I said. "It's to find out about the presence of drugs or poison in a dead person's blood at the time of death. Go ahead."

"Yeah, toximology test, or whatever, anyhow, they tell me the toxic test showed Tracy died of a heroin overdose and it's my fault 'cause I gave him the drug. Then they tell me my BP meds weren't BP meds at all, but high-grade heroin. I tell them to go to hell and to fuck right off, in those words, ain't nobody responsible for Tracy's death but Tracy, and I don't know nobody who would sell me that junk and they made a mistake. I don't possess horse and I never have. Well they don't like me telling them off like that, so they haul me down to the station. They're asking me questions for God knows how long, not letting me pee, freezing my nipples off. They're keeping the room colder than a witch's tit, which is bull, if you ask me."

I knew what she was talking about, and I thought it was nonsense as well. I knew why cops did it, but it didn't make it any less ethical. They were trying to get a confession from my mother in any way they could. They deliberately tried to make her uncomfortable to the extreme so she would confess to a crime just to get out of there.

My mother was talking way too fast and I wanted to slow her down.

"Mom, it's okay. You don't have to tell me the entire story right now. I'll be coming down to the jail within the next half-hour."

Nate and Amelia were home with Gretchen. I had arranged for Gretchen to watch the both of them. I needed to speak with the counselor completely alone because I needed her advice for what to do with Nate. Turned out that everything she was telling me about how I needed to slow down, maybe even take a sabbatical, would go right out the window. My mother was charged with murder. As much as my mother and I did not get along over the years, and we didn't get along over the years because of the way she was when I was growing up – drinking all the time, a revolving door of men, just basically being neglectful – I had forgiven her once I found out the reason she always had her own share of mental problems. She was raped by a very wealthy man, Josh Roland, and I was a result of that rape.

Josh Roland was then bludgeoned to death by an oriental lamp in his office and I was charged with his murder. It turned out the person who murdered him was Addison Weston, the First Lady of the State of Missouri. She had hired somebody to actually do the deed, Jaclyn Peterson, who ended up charged with manslaughter and was currently serving 10 years in prison for her role in the murder. As for Addison, she managed to be acquitted on the basis of temporary insanity. She hired the best attorney money could buy, which was why she got that result, while her patsy did the time Addison needed to. It was the best justice money could buy, which unfortunately was the way of the legal system. If you got money, you get away with anything. If you don't, you're going down no matter if you did it or not.

Now my mother was charged with murder. A nonsense charge if ever there was one. I had heard of people being charged with murder just because they were taking drugs with somebody who happened to die, and also instances where people were charged with murder because they bought drugs for somebody. But in this case, it was none of the above. My mom wasn't doing drugs with him, she just let him sleep on her couch. So she happened to be in the room when he died, and that makes her a murderer? Seriously?

Something was very off about this entire thing. To say the least. I would have to see her in jail and try to figure out what was going on. And then I would have to storm over to the prosecutor's office and find out what the hell they were thinking. How could they possibly charge my mother with murder for something so stupid?

Then I realized something. My mother was probably lying. She said didn't do drugs, but I knew she did. She also drank a lot. It was entirely possible that when they took a urinalysis at her home, after she called 911 about Tracy's death, they found out she had drugs in her system as well. And if they were the same drugs as those found in Tracy Dunham's system, they could charge her with murder. It would still be a baloney charge, but it would be a much more solid charge than if she was just sitting in her house when he came to visit, he passed out on her couch, he died and she had nothing to do with it.

I had a feeling there was more to the story than what she was telling me. He probably came over, the two of them started doing drugs, she went to bed, he did as well, and he was dead when she woke up. If that was the case, her urinalysis would prove that. If the UA showed opium in her system, then the state would have a much better case than if she was sober and just let him sleep on her couch.

I would definitely need to find out the results of my mother's drug test before I spoke with her. If the drug test showed she was clean when she was arrested, it would be no problem getting the case dismissed. I didn't know why they could charge her in this case unless there was something else I didn't know. At any rate, the prosecutors would have to drop the charges against her if she was clean at the time of the death because they couldn't win at trial unless they showed she supplied the drugs to him somehow. It would be an open and shut case and a waste of money for them.

I called Gretchen, told her what was going on, and then immediately headed down to the police station. I would get my mom's records, see what kind of questions they asked her in the interrogation room, and, most importantly, get the results of her urinalysis and see if she had drugs in her system.

I left the office building where I had been talking to Dr. Jordan, opened the door and a blast of cold hit me in the face. When I went to see Dr. Jordan, the weather had started to change from the 70° it had been earlier, dropping to around 50°. That was the one thing people always said about the weather in Missouri – if you don't like it, just wait a minute, and it'll change. And it certainly did on that day. It was early fall, October, and the leaves were just starting to change and fall from the trees.

I hugged my coat closer around my body as I made my way towards my Mercedes SUV in the parking lot. It was a new car for me, the one luxury I bought when I settled a large medical malpractice suit a few years back. In that case, it turned out the doctor who had given my client's son anesthesia that he was allergic to, did so deliberately. He was an angel of mercy, which was what he fashioned himself to be, for he was killing terminal patients. It turned out he had a son who had died slowly of cancer, going through much pain and agony along the way and didn't want anybody else to suffer that. So, when he got the records of his patients and found out they were terminal and were going in for surgery, he would deliberately give them the wrong anesthesia or too much anesthesia and they ended up dead. Everybody was entitled to punitive damages against him because he was doing intentional acts. I was the first in line, so I got a large settlement from him.

Once I got that $4 million settlement, I put most of it away for my kid's college and gave Harper a good percentage of it as well. I bought a new house, close to where Harper lived in the Brookside area, and this new Mercedes SUV. The rest of it, I squirreled away. After growing up poor, in a trailer, with a mother who didn't work and was constantly cycling men in and out of the home, I was constantly insecure that I would be poor again. No matter how much money I had, it would never be enough for me to feel like I would never be on skid row again.

I got to the jail and told the guard that I needed to see my mom's file. They knew me because I was there all the time, so they gave me her file without questioning me or asking me for an ID. I opened it up and immediately saw the results of my mother's blood test – she had tested positive for opiates. Also in the file were the results of the toxicology test they did for Tracy Dunham, and he too, had opiates in his system. Specifically, the results of the toxicology examination showed that the heroin in his system was high-grade and extremely pure.

It also looked like mom's "blood pressure" meds weren't actually blood pressure meds, but were heroin in a pill form. The officers indicated they had probable cause to seize the meds and test them because mom dropped a dirty UA and her companion had died of an apparent overdose. So the label on the pill bottle said Nifedipine, but it was actually heroin, according to the toxicology report on my mother's prescription BP pills.

I looked through the interrogation documents and saw my mom did not admit to doing anything except for what she told me – she told the cops that she was sitting in her trailer home, minding her own business, when Tracy came to her door. According to my mom, Tracy told her that he'd been thrown out by his wife, Priscilla. My mom then went to bed and woke up to find him dead. That's what she told the cops, over and over again. They never told her they knew she was lying and had opiates in her system at the time Tracy died.

It looked like I would have to confront my mother with her lie.

I went back up to the guard station and told them I was there to see Olivia Ward. The guard nodded. "Just a second, I'll let you through."

I went through the first set of double doors into the hallway, took the elevator up to the fifth floor which was where my mother was staying, went down the long corridor door and got to her pod. Once there, I rang the guards, and they let me through. I told the guard inside the waiting area that I was there to see Olivia Ward, the guard nodded her head, and told me to wait just a few minutes.

Mom came out a few minutes later, looking her usual self. She was down to about 100 pounds or less, and her hair, which was usually dark or bleached blonde, was currently pink. Or, rather, it was streaked pink. I could see her usual brunette hair peeking out from underneath the pink streaks, along with a lot of grey roots. She was dressed in an orange jumpsuit that absolutely hung from her skinny frame.

"God, I could use a smoke and a drink." She put her hands on the table, and they were shaking. It looked like she was going through the DTs, and I wouldn't be surprised if that was the case, as much as she drank. "I've been puking in this place. Nobody cares. Got the shakes so bad I feel like I'm going to rattle and roll right out of this joint."

"Mom," I said to her. "You tell me you need a smoke and a drink. And I'll be honest with you, you look like you're worse for the wear."

"I look like something the cat dragged in and I know it. You don't have to rub it in, kiddo."

"I'm not saying this to be mean. I do need to ask you a question, though. You told me over the phone that you weren't doing drugs with this Tracy Dunham person." I stopped my sentence right there, because I wanted to see her reaction to what I was going to say to her. I wanted to see what kind of facial expression and body language she displayed.

To my surprise, she didn't flinch. "Yeah, I told you that, because it's the God's honest truth. I told you I wasn't doing drugs with him, and that's what I mean. I was sitting in my trailer, minding my own damn business, and he came over and crashed on my couch." She narrowed her eyes at me. "Why do I think you think I'm lying? I got the sneaking suspicion that you're over there thinking I told you a tall tale."

I leaned forward. "Mom, I took a peek at your file before I came to see you. According to the file, there were opiates in your system at the time you were arrested. Heroin was also found in the bloodstream of the victim. You care to explain that?"

"Dammit. I told you I wasn't doing drugs with him. I told you I don't do drugs. I drink, I get shit-faced on that, I smoke a lot. I do weed. And that's it. No cocaine, no meth, no heroin, no hillbilly heroin, no nothing. I don't get into that crap. I know, I know, I used to do all that crap. All of it. But I gave it up about 10 years ago and I've never looked back. Drinking, smoking cigarettes, and smoking bud are all I do now."

"Mom, I don't believe you. If it's true what you're saying, why were opiates found in your system?"

"Hell, I don't know. You tell me."

I closed my eyes. "Mom, this is important. If there were not drugs in your system, there would be no way the prosecutor could possibly prove you were doing drugs with your friend Tracy. If they can't prove that, the whole case goes away unless they can prove you supplied Tracy with the heroin that killed him. I mean, they could still try to pursue charges, but it would be so easy to prove to the jury that you had nothing to do with his death that they would have to drop the charges. But if there was really heroin in your system, it'll be a little more difficult to get the charges dismissed."

She shook her head. "What is this bullcrap, anyway? Is that how it's going to be? You're doing drugs, somebody bites it and suddenly you're on the hook? I never heard of that."

"Unfortunately, it's not unheard of. All around the nation, people who were just doing drugs with another person who died are being found guilty, or at least charged, for their death. Usually, however, the charge is a murder only when somebody actually supplies the other person with the drugs. Regardless, it would be helpful if there were not drugs in your system."

"Is sounds like somebody was cooking the books here."

"What's that supposed to mean?"

"Just what it sounds like. Somebody doctored up my damn record and made it look like I was taking drugs when I wasn't. And you know when those pigs found drugs in my house, I knew for sure they're full of crap, because I damn well know I had no drugs at the house. Everything I said to you earlier on the phone is the God's honest truth. I didn't give that man no heroin, I didn't take no heroin with him, I had nothing to do with none of it, and I certainly didn't have no heroin in no prescription bottle."

I made a steeple with my hands, and stared at them for a minute or two. "Did you know Tracy was on drugs?"

"Hell no. I told you, me and him were sex buddies, nothing more, nothing less. We get together, drink and smoke weed, hit the sack, he'd leave. That was all there was to it."

"How did you meet him?"

She rolled her eyes. "At some fancy-schmancy thousand-dollar plate dinner. The governor himself was the guest of honor." She shook her head. "I met him at a dive bar. He asked me to dance, I said yes, we hit it off, he came back to my place, boom boom boom, that was that. No muss, no fuss."

"Do you remember the bar you met him at?"

"Why the hell does that matter? I don't remember which bar it was, probably someplace in Lee's Summit where the fake bikers go. You know the guys I'm talking about, the muckety-mucks who got full-time jobs as executives who like to ride their hogs on the weekends and act tough. A bunch of those fake bikers were hanging out at the bar that night. That's all I remember. I don't remember which bar it was."

I made notes as we spoke. "Was Tracy Dunham one of those fake bikers?"

She shrugged. "I suppose so. I don't really know. All I know is, I get up to go to the little girl's room to take a leak, and when I come back, there's a guy sitting at my barstool. Never seen the guy before in my whole life. It's crowded, there ain't no place to sit, and he's sitting in the one open seat. My seat. I even have my purse on the bar in front of him. I go to take my purse from the bar and try to find some other place to sit. He just looks at me, drags on his cigarette, tells me to sit on his lap. I ain't in the mood for that, I tell him to go to hell. He keeps going, says he wants to buy me a drink because he took my seat. I say why not? Free drink, all I got to do is hang out with the guy. So I did. I hung out with him. Got my free drink. Free drink turned into about six more, next thing I know, we're back in my dump screwing around. He leaves, I figure I'm never gonna see him again, but he pops back in a couple weeks later, and it just kind of went like that. He'd come over like a booty call and I let him come over like a booty call. I didn't know nothing about him, he didn't know nothing about me. That was how I liked it. He liked it too."

"Okay. So you knew nothing about this guy. You don't even know if he was doing drugs on a regular basis."

"Yeah, that's right. Why do you keep asking me these questions like you don't believe what I'm telling you? Listen, you've always been a shit to me. You've never trusted me any further than you can throw me. But I'm telling you the God's honest truth right now. I knew nothing about that guy."

"What else can you tell me?"

She shrugged. "I told you everything I can tell you. Everything I'm gonna tell you. You can either believe me or not, but I'm telling you what I know."

I tapped my fingers on the table, wondering why I had a nagging feeling there was much more to the story than what she was telling me. There was something behind this case. Something I wasn't seeing, and maybe my mother wasn't seeing either. I just wished she knew something more about this guy. I believed her when she said she didn't know anything about him, however. My mother was just that kind of person. She had sex with men she didn't know and didn't always get their backgrounds or histories. She wasn't somebody who would even get a person's last name all the time.

"Okay, then. I guess I'll talk to the prosecutor's office and find out why they're doing this to you. Maybe I can glean something from them. In the meantime, you just sit tight, and I'll try to figure out what's going on. I guess your initial appearance is tomorrow, so I'll try to get a bond for you."

She shrugged. "Do what you gotta do. God knows I'm not going nowhere anytime soon. I'll see you tomorrow."

---

AS I DROVE HOME that night, I thought about what my mother was telling me in the jail. I didn't doubt her story, but at the same time, what was up with her file saying she had heroin in her system? Did somebody really falsify that record, and if they did, why would they do something like that? And who would do something like that?

Something was fishy, and I would find out what exactly it was.

## Until Proven Guilty: Chapter Three

I GOT HOME a little bit after 10 PM and went straight to Nate's room to see what he was doing.

He was sitting at his desk, looking at his computer, apparently playing a video game. He didn't look in my direction when I came in the door, so I went over to him and put my hands on his shoulders and squeezed them lightly. "Hey, buddy. How are things going?"

He shrugged and said nothing.

I sat on the bed. I waited for him to turn around and look at me, but he kept on playing his game. I remembered what my therapist, Dr. Jordan, told me – she told me not to be discouraged if Nate didn't want to open up, but to not let him shut me out.

Without turning around, he said "Dad, you were supposed to be home hours ago. You promised you would be home tonight after you talked to our therapist."

I took a deep breath. "Nate, I know what I said this morning. But something came up with your grandmother. She's in trouble. A lot of trouble."

Nate finally turned around, his green eyes looking haunted. "What kind of trouble?"

I debated about how much I wanted to tell him about what was going on with my mother. Nate was very close with my mother and always had been. Even when I went through a period of time when I didn't want to talk to her, he would always ask about her, asking when she would come and visit them. My daughter Amelia felt the same way about her. Both kids would be upset when they found out about my mother being charged with murder.

It was such a precarious time with Nate. I hesitated to say anything to him.

"She's just having a problem. I really wanted to be home tonight with you guys, make you dinner, watch movies with you, just hang out. I had every intention of coming home right at six, and I would have if I didn't have to see my mother."

Nate turned back around and started playing with his video game again. "It's okay, Dad. Really, it's okay."

The way he said that made me know it really wasn't okay. I just had the sinking feeling that I was losing him. I remembered my own childhood, how I was going down the wrong path, stealing cars, smoking and drinking when I was ten, the same age Nate was now, generally getting into trouble and raising hell. Once I got out of prison for a crime I didn't commit, I swore I would turn my life around completely and no child of mine would go the route I did. Yet, here was Nate, shutting me out, shutting out the world, and I didn't know how to reach him. I didn't know what he needed from me. He wasn't telling me.

I felt adrift.

"No, Nate. It's not okay. It's not okay that I told you one thing and then went back on my word. You can tell me, buddy. You can talk to me. You can tell me anything on your mind and I want you to. If you hate me, I want you to tell me that. If you're angry, tell me. Don't be shy."

What was ironic was that his sister, Amelia, was the opposite of him. She told me anything and everything, and if she was mad, I knew it. She didn't mince words, even though she was only 9 years old. She had stared down death and beat it. She told the Grim Reaper *not today asshole*, and that gave her the kind of strength to face anything life threw her way. She was tested by her battle with cancer, and by how close she came to death's door, and she came out the other side.

In a way, Nate was tested along with her. He suffered right along with her. True, he didn't go through all she went through – the infections, the nausea, the pain, the fatigue, the fear. The constant tests, the stays in the hospital. He didn't actually go through those things. But he was a very sensitive boy, so he absorbed her pain. When she hurt, he did as well. I knew that.

He just shrugged. "It's late, Dad. I gotta get to bed."

I stood up and squeezed his shoulders and tousled his hair. "You're right. I'll see you in the morning."

I turned away, closing the door behind me. Before I went to bed, I went to Amelia's room and checked on her. She was fast asleep, so I went down to my own room, sat on the bed, and thought about things.

I thought about what my therapist, Dr. Jordan, told me about how I was supposed to deal with Nate. I realized that was just not possible. Until I got my mom out of this jam, there was nothing I could really do but work her case and make sure she got the best representation possible. I didn't trust her case in anybody else's hands.

I called Harper. It was late, I knew that, but I knew she

usually stayed up late working on her cases. I had a feeling she wouldn't be too upset with me if I called her.

She answered on the third ring. She sounded like she had been crying. "What's going on, Damien?"

"Nothing." I took a deep breath. To tell the truth, I didn't know why I was calling her. I guess I just needed someone to talk to, a sounding board. I had been seeing, off and on, Ally Hughes from the prosecutor's office. It wasn't anything serious, and she wasn't necessarily somebody I could call and talk to when I was feeling out of sorts. Yet Harper and I had become close friends and confidants, as well as being partners in our law firm.

She sniffled on the phone. "It's not nothing, the reason why you called. Something must be going on. You don't ever call me this time of night. So tell me what's up."

I took a deep breath. "Are the girls in bed? I'd really like to come over. My kids are asleep, but I can have the neighbor girl, Gretchen, come over and watch them. She does that sometimes when I need her at night." She didn't mind it. There were times when I would go out late at night and she would sleep on the couch or in the guest bedroom. I only had her come over because I didn't entirely trust my two young children to be home alone. And the great thing about Gretchen was that she lived close by so she could come over at just about any time. At a moment's notice. And she liked it, because I paid her a lot more when she came over on an emergency basis.

Harper sniffled again, and coughed. "Yeah, the girls are in bed. Come on over. In fact, I'm glad you called. I really didn't want to be alone tonight."

"Why? Is there something going on?"

She cleared her throat. "Axel and I are not seeing each other anymore. He broke up with me tonight."

*Oh, crap.* Harper and Axel had been dating for a long time and were very serious and in love. I liked Axel a lot and I knew he was really a part of Harper's family. Harper would no doubt be devastated.

"Oh, I'm so sorry to hear that. What happened?" I asked.

Harper cleared her throat and caught a sob. "He's going back to Australia because he's being deported. I thought he was a permanent resident, even a citizen. I mean, he's been in the states for a long time. He told me he'd tried to become a permanent resident, but his brother Daniel had already been deported to Australia because of his drug problems. Because of his brother's problems, Axel broke the law to make sure his brother didn't go to prison. He covered up his brother's drug problems by taking some evidence out of the evidence room at the police department. His brother would've gone to prison for life, because he was busted with a lot of drugs, and the Feds would have to get involved, so Axel went into the evidence room and destroyed the evidence that would've been used against Daniel. The KCPD had to drop the charges against Daniel after that. I guess Axel finally got caught, so now he's being deported."

I listened to Harper without a word. I knew what she was going through. I had gone through my share of broken hearts myself. My most recent broken heart was when I divorced my wife, Sarah.

Sarah was not a good person. Granted, she had gone through a lot in her life – her father committed suicide, her brother died of cancer when she was young, not six months after her father committed suicide, and her mother had a hard time trying to pick up the pieces with just the two of them. So, in a way, I had a lot of sympathy for her. Even though she abandoned Amelia and me when we needed her the most, when Amelia was on death's door, and I really thought we would have say goodbye to her, I still felt sorry for Sarah. During that time, Sarah was not only not around, she was fighting me every step of the way. She wanted to stop Amelia's treatment. She thought it wasn't doing her any good and our daughter was only suffering on our behalf. I was of the mind that we had to do everything we could to make sure Amelia survived. I felt that if I didn't do everything in my power, I would have a lot of regrets if she ended up dying. Turned out the last thing I did was the thing that actually saved her, so I didn't regret putting Amelia through all those years of torture.

That was bad enough, but when Sarah tried to terminate my parental rights to Amelia, just because she wanted her new boyfriend to get his inheritance money, and he wasn't entitled to it unless he had a child, it was the final straw. Sarah claimed her new boyfriend was Amelia's biological father and doctored up a paternity test to prove it. It turned out I wasn't Amelia's biological father. Yet, I was able to not have my rights severed because the biological father also was not Sarah's boyfriend. It was another guy, a guy who didn't want to be named the biological father of Amelia. Because of that, I beat the case that Sarah filed against me to have my rights terminated to Amelia. It was a long way back, psychologically, for Amelia and me after that.

I couldn't forgive Sarah for doing that to us.

And that, truth be told, was why I was reluctant to get close with Ally. She was a beautiful girl, very smart and capable, and we had a lot of fun together. But I was held back by my general lack of trust in women. If Sarah was capable of doing something like that to me, who knows what somebody else might do to me? I trusted Sarah completely and she burned me in the worst way possible.

I drove over to Harper's house, and she greeted me on her front porch.

"Come on in," she said to me. "I'm glad you came by. I'm glad you could come over and talk. I've been sitting here in a dark room, trying to imagine what's going to happen to me now. Axel was the first man I've been able to be with since my teenage years. He's been the first man I've been able to trust. I've never let a man into my heart until him. Now I just worry that everything will be sown back up. That my heart will be blocked again."

I looked at her glass and saw it had an amber liquid in it. I felt more than a little concerned about it. Harper was a recovering alcoholic and had been off the wagon a time or two in the recent past. I had to hope and pray she was not drinking again.

I sniffed at her glass and smelled the unmistakable odor of bourbon.

I put my arm around her. "Harper," I said, as gently as I could. "Is that whiskey in that glass?"

She shrugged. "What of it?"

I took a deep breath, not knowing how to handle the situation. I had been around my mother as she was trying to quit drinking several times and it never took. But I knew Harper had really wanted to not go back to drinking. I knew how much she struggled. I knew she had gone to AA, and had a sponsor, whose name was Crystal Warner. She had several sponsors over the years and Crystal was her current one.

"I understand you're hurting but you have a couple of children to think about. They'll be affected if you're drinking again. You need to think of them."

She shook her head. "I just don't know, Damien. Sometimes I think I just can't handle life. Just can't face it. I thought that when Axel and I were good, he would always be there for me. Hold me up when I'm down. He was my person. And now he's gone. Deported to Australia. I'm never going to see him again."

Harper was not a woman who felt sorry for herself a lot of the time. She was always somebody, in my eyes, who carried on no matter what happened to her. Yet it seemed she was breaking down.

She shook her head as she took a sip of her bourbon. "It's just one. I can handle it. It's just one."

I was very concerned, because that was what all addicts say. They say it's just the one, they can handle it, they don't really have a problem. But that was a lie. It was a lie all addicts tell themselves and the world. And I didn't really know what to do. I could never stop my mom from drinking. As much as I tried to stop her from drinking when I was younger, she never would.

And now, here my mother was, being charged with murder. And what she did to be charged with murder was a nonsense charge, but that didn't matter. In a way, her drinking led her to where she was at the moment – sitting in a cell. If she wasn't such a drinker, she would have never been at the bar where she met that Tracy Dunham, and if she never would've met Tracy Dunham, she would never have been charged with his murder.

I didn't know what to say to Harper, so I decided to change the subject. "Thanks for seeing me. I was feeling out of sorts because of what's going on with Nate, and my mother –"

She nodded. "After you told me your mother was being charged with murdering Tracy Dunham, I did a little bit of research on him. Bet you didn't know his family is very well-connected and very wealthy. Came as a surprise to me too, because of what you said about him. Sounded to me like he was just kind of a drifter and loser. I don't know, I guess that was just my own prejudice showing. Whenever I hear of people dying of a heroin overdose, I always think they're people on the fringes of society. People who don't have it all together. This guy was not only from a wealthy family, but was a medical doctor."

A medical doctor? His family was rich and powerful? I guessed that made a certain kind of perverse sense to me, considering my mother said she met him in a fake biker bar where professionals hung out and tried to pretend they were hog-riders. It sounded like Tracy Dunham was one of those fakers who probably wore leather jackets and dark sunglasses while hanging out at a biker bar trying to look cool. I doubted he even could find Sturgis on a map, let alone attend an annual rally.

"That's interesting to hear," I said to her. "What kind of medical doctor was he?"

She laughed ruefully and took another sip of her bourbon. "You want one?" she asked me, gesturing with her glass.

I shook my head. "No," I said, not wanting to encourage or enable her. "Thank you."

"Suit yourself," she said. "It's the good stuff. Pappy Van Winkle 20- year reserve. Smooth as molasses, this one is. The better stuff doesn't give me as much of a hangover, either." She took another sip and seemed to forget the question I just asked her.

"Thanks," I said. "Now…" I cleared my throat. "What kind of doctor was Tracy Dunham?"

She nodded. "Dr. Tracy Dunham was the best kind of

doctor there was if you've been in a bad car accident or skiing mishap and are in excruciating pain. His specialty was pain management." She laughed. "Ironic, huh? You would think a guy like that could substitute Hillbilly Heroin for the real thing. I wonder why he got high on street junk like that, let alone take so much that he overdosed."

"Hillbilly Heroin" was the street slang for Oxycodone, a powerful opioid.

A doctor taking heroin made little sense to me, either. Harper was right. A doctor would have access to Oxycontin, Fentanyl, Codeine, Hydrocodone, anything he would want to get high.

Then again, once I thought about it, I realized he probably was trying to hide his drug use and addiction, and there's only so much a doctor can do to legally obtain painkillers. Even a pain management doctor. He couldn't legally use his own scrip pad to write himself a prescription. He would have access to free samples sent by pharmaceutical companies, but not Opioids, which were Schedule III drugs, therefore pharma reps cannot give them out as samples. He no-doubt received drugs his patients might bring to his office for disposal, but he needed to properly dispose of them according to law.

So, unless he was actually diagnosed with a condition that would warrant him being prescribed pain meds, he wouldn't have legal access to them.

"I don't think he could get pain meds legally, even if he was a doctor," I said.

She nodded. "Huh. How naive are you?"

I took a deep breath, not liking where this conversation was going. I didn't like Harper's attitude, either. She seemed colder, more bitter, more cynical than usual. Harper wasn't exactly the warmest woman on the planet, even on a good day, but at the moment she seemed to be just a bit icy. "Harper, maybe this was a mistake, my coming here."

"A mistake?" She shook her head. "I did you a solid, finding out about your victim. I know you didn't know that about him, although you probably should have. Wasn't his occupation in the file you read before you went to see your mother?"

"I don't recall seeing that," I said. "But, then again, I skimmed that file. I was just looking to see if my mother was high at the time he showed up at her door."

"Well, let's see," Harper said. "Something is clearly amiss in this case. I don't know what, but something clearly is. Your mother insisted to you, up and down, that she didn't take a single drug that night. Yet opiates were found in her system. Tracy Dunham wasn't a rando drug user off the street. He was a physician and his family is rich. The cops interrogated your mother as if she were high and Dunham was a rando, but they had to have known at the time that this just wasn't true. It sounds like they never even pressed the issue of Dunham's occupation when they were questioning your mother. Why do you think that's the case? Add to that the fact that they have such a hard-on for poor Olivia in the first place, and I think you can agree something clearly rotten in the state of Denmark on this one."

"Well, that goes without saying," I said. "And I would imagine I'll figure out just what happened in this case. I usually do. And I thank you for doing the research on it."

"Not a problem," she said. "After Axel dumped me, I went looking for something to do to clear my mind and decided to try to solve your mother's case. Because I know you have more important things on your mind and don't need to be worrying about whether or not your mother will end up thrown in the clink."

I rocked in the porch chair for a few minutes, while Harper sipped her bourbon. I looked up at the sky, noticing that it was clear with a visible blanket of stars. A man walking his dog ambled up the sidewalk and the dog lifted his leg on Harper's bush while the man rapidly walked past.

"Harper," I finally said. "I'm concerned about you."

"Why?" she asked. "Because of this?" She lifted her glass of bourbon and then brought it to her lips again. "Most people don't stay on the wagon, you know. It's too difficult. Sometimes you go for so long and then you get triggered and thirsty and you just can't help yourself. It's there, it's a friend, it's always been the one thing that can you make you feel good when you feel worthless. And that's what I feel - worthless. I just can't seem to not screw up my life, no matter what I do. So I drink. I drink to drown out those feelings."

She looked up at the stars and it was her turn to get silent.

"Harper-"

"My rapist is out of prison," she said, not looking at me. She brought her hand to her mouth and wiped it. "His lawyer proved ineffective assistance of counsel, no problem. While he was at it, he almost got my bar license. I had to do some pretty creative maneuvering and butt-kissing to keep my license after what I did to Michael Reynolds."

**Grab your copy...**
**vinci-books.com/provenguilt**

## About the Author

Rachel Sinclair was a criminal defense attorney for eleven years, so she doesn't scare easily. She graduated from the University of Missouri-Kansas City School of Law in 1998, and worked for the Public Defender's Office for several years before striking out on her own. She currently lives in San Diego, California, with her boyfriend, Joey, and her two fur babies, Annie and Toby. In her spare time, she likes to read, bicycle all over town, Boogie Board at the beach, and watch trashy television.

www.ingramcontent.com/pod-product-compliance
Lightning Source LLC
LaVergne TN
LVHW030241250326
834688LV00047B/1752